I0548209

ECHO ACADEMY - SPECIAL EXTENDED EDITION

BOOK FOUR OF THE DIMENSION DRIFT SERIES

CHRISTINA BAUER

CONTENTS

ECHO ACADEMY

ALSO BY CHRISTINA BAUER

NEW APPENDIX OF TOTALLY AWESOME GOODIES

STANDARD APPENDIX OF STUFF THAT'S STILL PRETTY COOL

COPYRIGHT

Monster House Books
Brighton, MA 02135
ISBN 9781945723483
First Edition

Copyright © 2020 by Monster House Books LLC
All rights reserved. This book or any portion thereof may not be reproduced or used in any manner whatsoever without the express written permission of the publisher except for the use of brief quotations in a book review.

For every crap boss who inspired me to leave the software industry and
become a full-time writer.
You know who you are.
Nyah nyah nyah NYAH nyah.

COLLECTED WORKS
CHRISTINA BAUER

Dimension Drift
Dystopian adventures with science, snark, and hot aliens
1. Scythe
2. Umbra
3. Alien Minds
4. ECHO Academy
5. Justice
6. Slate

Angelbound Origins
About a quasi (part demon and part human) girl who loves kicking butt in Purgatory's Arena
1. Angelbound
2. Scala
3. Acca
4. Thrax
5. The Dark Lands
6. The Brutal Time
7. Armageddon
8. Quasi Redux
9. Clockwork Igni
10. Lady Reaper

Angelbound Offspring
The next generation takes on Heaven, Hell, and everything in between
1. Maxon

ECHO ACADEMY

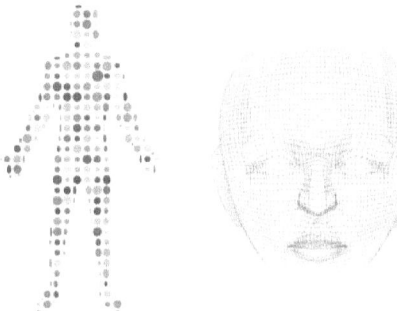

PREFACE

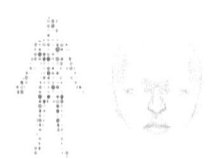

*ECHO ACADEMY begins with an expanded scene from the previous novel,
ALIEN MINDS.*

1 / MEIMI

I STAND on an almost-empty street of the planet Umbra.

That's right.

Not Earth.

Umbra.

This isn't one of my science books or simulations either. I, Meimi Archer, have journeyed to a completely different planet, solar system, galaxy, blabbity blah.

It all went by in a flash. I left a party, stepped into a drift void, and—WHOOSH—now I'm here. Taking in a deep breath, I seek to truly process that fact.

Total fail.

So I check my outfit instead.

My frilly pink dress is ruined. Meh.

Clothing isn't normally my thing. I'm more of a dark matter and quantum particles type gal. But in this moment? A trashed outfit feels super easy to face. The alien planet situation? Not so much. Plus, there's an evil space cowboy lurking nearby who happens to be Emperor of the Omniverse.

I'm not even kidding.

And did I mention how his Imperial Dudeness wants to kill my boyfriend, Thorne, who's the only other person around? Yup, that's happening, too.

Ding, ding, ding!

An internal alert goes off in my noggin, saying it's time to re-examine the hem of my gown again. Yup, still matted up with dirt and prairie grass. And is that a dead bug under the lace? Ick.

Get a grip, Meimi. You're here to help Thorne.

It takes a great force of will, but I sideline my clothing analysis and scan my surroundings. Ahead of me stretches a thin street flanked by wooden buildings. Names like *saloon* and *sheriff* are written on the facades in chipped paint. All the water troughs are rotted out. A broken shutter bangs in the wind. Basically, it's your classic deserted town of the Old West variety.

Down the road stands Thorne, Prince of Umbra and general hottie in black body armor. He's my age—around eighteen—with dark hair, blue eyes and a warrior's build. Plus he has dimples. That's an issue. In the end, I blame that smile for why I hauled my cookies across the universe to help fight Cole, the thug who's more than Thorne's attacker or emperor.

Cole also happens to be Thorne's father.

I know. Twisted.

Speaking of the emperor, Cole stands a towering seven feet tall, making him a mountain of a man with rough skin and cropped gray hair. He sports a Stetson, eye patch, leather pants and heavy boots... and all that the emperor wears is black as midnight.

No false packaging with this guy.

Cole narrows his eyes in my direction. "Welcome to Umbra." He tips his Stetson. With that movement, the hat bursts into a small dust cloud before disappearing back into Cole's flesh.

This isn't a magic trick; Cole wields powerful nanoparticles called Crown Sentient. That's the *killer* part of my *killer cowboy* situation. Regular sentient help all Umbrans travel through space, fight battles, see the future, you name it. But Crown Sentient do all that on steroids... and only for the emperor.

"Here's where you'll die," Cole adds.

I roll my eyes. *Like that idea didn't occur to me already.*

"No!" Thorne rounds on his father. "Keep your word. This is *our* fight. Meimi stays free."

Cole snarls out a single word. "Maybe."

No question what that means. Cole plans to murder us both. My stupor instantly vanishes. Obsessing about dresses? That was so forty seconds ago. Right now, I have a single thought.

Save the prince.

Hoisting up my skirts, I race toward Thorne.

Ten yards.

Moving with impossible speed, Cole throws dozens of rapid punches at his son's skull, ribs and kidneys. Thorne counters just as quickly, blocking each attack. Cole pauses, barely winded. Meanwhile Thorne braces his arms on his knees as he catches his breath.

Five yards away now.

"Son," declares Cole. "This is getting on my nerves." A cloud of particles appears around Cole's right arm. The next instant, those dark sentient solidify into a long Winchester rifle. Fear prickles across my skin. Cole raises the weapon, aims at Thorne, and fires.

BOOM!

The bullet strikes Thorne squarely in the chest. My guy gets thrown across the street, through a glass window, and into a building marked *saloon*.

I do a double take.

Triple take.

The emperor's super-powerful alien gun just blasted my boyfriend across a street. That's not something you see every day, even on a movie feed. My pulse moves into hyper drive. Cole talks a big game about killing his son.

Did he just murder Thorne?

Scanning the broken window, Cole rests his rifle on his shoulder. "Bet you didn't know Crown Sentient could do that, eh?"

My body turns numb with shock. Everyone knows what guns can do. And super-charged Crown Sentient guns? It's only logical that Cole's weapon would pack more power.

To me, the rifle isn't what's shocking... it's the fact that Cole is Thorne's *father*.

And the emperor shows zero concern that Thorne may be hurt. Worry twists through me.

Thorne could even be dead.

Cole speeds across the dirt road. I rush behind the emperor, following him into the empty saloon. Overturned tables and chairs cover the floor. A booze counter stands stocked with broken bottles. Wind tinkles random keys on a busted player piano. It's creepy as all get out.

Thorne sits against the far wall. The wood behind him buckles from the force of his spine having slammed onto the panel. He twitches; I freeze.

Thorne's alive. *Yes!*

What I see next makes my heart sink. With every breath, Thorne's lungs gurgle ominously. Splatters of blood line the nearby wall and floor.

Oh, no. Thorne's dying.

This can't be happening.

Cole saunters over to Thorne and stops. Raising his right arm, the emperor points his rifle toward Thorne's face. Cole then launches into a long list of my guy's execution-worthy crimes. All the while, that rifle stays jammed against Thorne's cheek.

No time to lose.

I'm so done watching Cole beat up my boyfriend. Time to take things into my own hands. Literally. Reaching into my dress pocket, I pull out a small container which contains swarm sentient, a variety that forms something far better than a shotgun. Not that this is a big space competition for who has the best stuff.

It's more of a science fair.

In any case, I plan to win.

Swarm sentient can take a unified shape that includes a central consciousness. Basically, I've got more of a killer pet than a boring old gun. My particular swarm becomes a semi-transparent creature called the Lacerator. And it's as badass as its name.

I open the container.

Sentient particles seep out of the tiny box, congealing into the shape of a semi-solid monster that towers seven feet tall. The Lacerator has a wide chest, stout legs, and empty holes serve as its eyes. Dinosaur-style spikes protrude from its spine. Razor-sharp teeth line its overly wide mouth.

Who cares if this swarm looks like a *connect the dots* dinosaur? My Lacerator is just the best.

Pictures appear in my mind—that's how the Lacerator communicates. Based on the images, the monster clearly wants me to issue a command.

That's easy.

"Heal Thorne," I order. "NOW."

The Lacerator bursts into a cloud of particles. The sight reminds me of a miniature tornado as it whirls across the saloon floor. Broken chairs and tattered playing cards get caught in the motion. Bands of fear tighten around my rib cage. I just ordered the Lacerator to cure Thorne, but that's more of a *hope* than anything else. I haven't actually seen the Lacerator do anything but kill stuff. My breath catches.

Can a sentient swarm fix a bullet wound?

The swarm slams into Thorne's chest. Dark particles swirl across my guy's arms, neck and face, forming moving tattoos of pinwheel-type lines. The ink-like markings seep right into Thorne's flesh, merging with his body. The scientist part of me thinks that's cool tech. The girlfriend side just wants to be Thorne not-nearly-dead already.

What happens next takes place in seconds, but forever seems to eke by as color returns to Thorne's skin. His bruises fade. Blood dries up and vanishes. After shaking his head, Thorne hops to his feet. Now that's a recovery sign if I've ever seen one.

I exhale. *Chalk up one for our side.*

"Well done, Meimi," says Thorne. Even his dimpled smile is back.

I give him a mock curtsey because one, I'm wearing a dress; and two, it's never a bad time for sass.

Cole staggers backward, the sentient rifle vanishing from his hands. The emperor's face pales with shock. "What?" Cole points at my nose. "Humans can't order sentient around."

"Well, I just did," I retort. "Get used to it."

Cole raises his arms. Once more, black particles swirl around his hands. This time, the Crown Sentient congeal into the shape of a lasso that's held tightly in the emperor's fist. With a snap of his wrist, the rope whips out from Cole's grip.

And it heads in my direction.

Thorne races toward me. "Get down, Meimi!"

There isn't time. One moment, I'm standing free. The next, a line of rope encircles my throat. I try to gulp in fresh air. *Useless.* The rough lasso bites into my skin.

Yet it also calls to my soul.

What happens next is pure instinct. Seconds ago, I communicated with the Lacerator using mental images. Now I send out a new command to the Crown Sentient around my neck. With all my focus, I imagine the lasso merging into my body.

Nothing happens.

I writhe to get free. The skin on my throat chafes and bleeds. My lungs ache for air. Once again, I picture the lasso melting into the same swirling markings I just saw on Thorne.

Again, there is no response.

Will the Crown Sentient ever act?

Suddenly the emperor's lasso bursts into a haze of particles. Hope sparks in my chest. *It's working!* There's a tickling sensation as markings appear on my throat, followed by a zing of electricity against my skin. No doubt, the Crown Sentient just merged into my body, the same as they did to Thorne.

Power thrums through my nervous system. Every corner of my soul vibrates with energy. Pain sears into my skull. It strikes me that I'm experiencing the worst *ice cream headache* of my life, times ten. The agony ends as quickly as it began. One fact appears with absolute certainty. I've taken in Crown Sentient.

Feels pretty good.

"How can this be?" Cole staggers backward. "You're not Umbran. And even if you were, no one but the emperor can take in Crown Sentient."

I bob my brows. "Oh, say it's impossible again. I love it." An idea appears. "How about this?"

For my next feat of amazingness, I imagine Thorne taking in Crown Sentient as well. With the picture firmly in mind, I raise my hand. Sure enough, Crown Sentient rise from my palm and race across the room. Fast as a whip, the sentient encompass Thorne in what looks like a dust cloud before turning into the same swirly markings as before. Those inky lines quickly seep into Thorne's chest, hands and mouth.

"This isn't happening," thunders Cole. "That boy is too weak."

"Maybe you need to expand your definition of what it means to be strong," counters Thorne.

I shoot him a thumbs-up. *Good point there, alien boyfriend.*

Cole forms his Winchester again. I suppose he thinks that's a menacing move, but I have another thought entirely.

More Crown Sentient for us, yum yum.

Reaching forward, I summon those particles to me as well. The rifle instantly dissolves into dark specks that fly across the saloon and soak directly into my body. Fresh waves of energy flow though my nervous system. The ice cream headache returns for a few seconds, but I can ignore it better this time.

The emperor scowls at Thorne. "I don't need sentient to fight you." Cole lunges for his son. This time, when the emperor attacks his child, Thorne does more than just block the blows.

He hits back.

One strike.

Two.

Three.

With Thorne's last punch, Cole flies across the room. The emperor lands against a back panel with an ear-splitting thunk. It occurs to me that Cole takes the same position Thorne did a few minutes ago—sitting against the wall with the panel behind him all busted up. The emperor looks unconscious, but you never know. I send out my own sentient to tie him up, just to be sure.

For a long second, I can only stare at the bound-up emperor. "Did we really do it?"

"Looks like," says Thorne. "I've never seen him knocked out before."

Some small part of me says this is too easy. But I decide to ignore that part, mostly because Thorne is racing toward me at a run. Soon our bodies press together in the mother of all hugs. Thorne's hand slides up the side of my torso and neck, ending with a firm grip on my chin.

I know what's coming next, and I love this idea.

Sometimes, it's good to be me.

"When you love someone across multiple realities, that connection can seep into your home world. Earthers call this finding your soul mate. On the planet Umbra, we say you discover your transcendent." - Empress Ophelia, author of *The Lost Book of Transcendence*

AT LAST, Meimi Archer is in my arms. For a moment, I soak in her perfection. Brown hair frames her heart-shaped face. Sixteen beloved freckles scatter across the bridge of her nose. The twin fires of intelligence and courage burn in her wide emerald eyes. She's seventeen and an immortal beauty, all at once.

Meimi's my transcendent—the woman I love in so many realities, it bleeds through into this one. Growing up, I thought transcendence was a myth.

Then I met Meimi.

I'm one lucky prince.

Little by little, I guide Meimi's lips toward mine. Once our mouths almost touch, I pause. Nothing compares to Meimi's kisses; I wish to commit this moment to memory. There's the way her lips glisten with a liquid beauty. How Meimi's soft curves press against my firm body. And the quick breaths which mean she wants this as much as I do.

For the hundredth time, I imagine our future. Such mental pictures kept me sane all those months when Meimi's memory was wiped and she didn't know me. Now those cherished images flood back.

There's Meimi and I riding hoverbikes across Umbra's prairies...

Waltzing on our wedding day...

And cradling our newborn.

I even see grey-haired versions of us cuddling on a porch swing, our faces wrinkled and happy.

Meimi goes up on her tiptoes. Our lips meet in a gentle kiss that's all things loving and grateful. But this isn't the time for much intimacy. Father won't stay passed out forever.

Meimi breaks the kiss. "What happens next?"

I let out a long breath. There's no question what Meimi refers to here.

Cole.

Fresh pictures flip through my brain. These aren't hoped-for futures; they're memories from a painful past. First come recollections of Father, a kind man who never treated me as less just because I didn't wield much sentient. Second follows thoughts of Cole, the emperor who rages and strikes. Crown Sentient fray Cole's mind, transforming a good man into an angry demon. Every week, Mother asks me to put Cole out of his misery. But I can't. There are still signs of the good man who is my father.

Even now, I just can't give up on Father yet. *How do I explain that to Meimi?*

"It's a good question," I begin.

"Why do I get the feeling this is a complex situation?"

"Because you'd be right. You should know the true choices here."

For a few seconds, Meimi stares at Cole. When her gaze meets mine again, my girl is all steely resolve. "Tell me everything."

"We could kill my father, take all his Crown Sentient, and become rulers of the omniverse. That's how Cole got the job."

"Honestly? I'm not a fan of becoming an alien emperor and empress right now."

"Same here. But I wanted to be honest. And there is another option."

"Let's hear it."

"I could take Cole back to my family's home at Fort Derringer. That's on the other side of the planet. Now that I can wield some of my father's Crown Sentient, maybe I can help him." I huff out a breath. "I have to try."

Meimi gently rests her palm against my cheek. "I understand."

Pure adoration pulses through my veins. *This girl.*

"I should get back then, I suppose."

My mind races. Truth is, I'd love to take Meimi to Fort Derringer, but it would be a big risk. For my people, knowing transcendents exist would be a major revelation. Then there's the fact that Meimi and I could be the next emperor and empress—that's not what people are expecting.

And when surprises do happen, the situation often ends in violence. Just because my family rules, doesn't mean we're without enemies.

"I would love to bring you to Fort Derringer one day," I say solemnly. "But when that happens, I want to ensure you'll be safe and welcomed. That might take some time."

"So to be together, we must be apart?" She shakes her head yet smiles. "That sounds like my luck."

"It won't be long. Soon you'll wield your sentient like a pro. We'll visit each other's worlds often." I glance over to Cole. "But that's the future. Right now, he could wake up any moment. It's time for us both to go home."

Just saying those words tears at my soul, but it's the truth. Meimi always deserves honesty.

"I'm not worried," says Meimi bravely. "I'll track you down in no time."

"Looking forward to it." Leaning forward, I rest my forehead against hers. A weight of sorrow hangs about us, heavy as the threat of rain.

Best to get this over with.

We step apart. Raising my right hand, I call upon the regular sentient power inside me. Silver particles lift from my palm as I create a circular transport portal called a drift void. Within seconds, a plate of gray specks hangs in the air.

Somehow, I force out the next five words. "You can step through now."

Meimi sighs. "Right."

My transcendent sets her fingers against the silver plate. Inch by inch, she glides her right arm into the whirl of gray. The sentient panel expands, ready to accept her entire body. Meimi steps in half-way. All the while, emotions pour through our transcendent bond.

I sense Meimi's bone-deep chill of despair.

The heat of her frustration.

And a shock of fear.

The sorrow of our farewell vanishes. Every muscle in my body goes on alert. *Something's scaring Meimi.* Sure enough, a presence looms behind me. No question who it is, either.

Cole has awoken.

"Goodbye," snarls the emperor. "Enjoy your exile."

The sentient surrounding Meimi do something I've never seen before.

Change color.

Particles of gray become tiny points of crimson. I blink, not believing what I'm seeing. *Red sentient.* These are illegal—even to the emperor—because they don't just transport someone to another part of the universe. They block both sides of that void, eternally.

No, no, no.

Cole is permanently separating Earth from Umbra... and me from Meimi.

On reflex, I reach out to my transcendent. Our fingertips almost brush. With the barest flash of crimson light, the red sentient disappear. Meimi vanishes as well. My mind blanks with shock. I reach out to Meimi through our bond. No flow of emotion pulses through. We're severed.

Yet my transcendent can't be gone. I won't allow it.

Focus, Thorne.

Minutes ago, Cole wanted to kill us both. Now he's fine with an exile void? Father is a rage machine, but that doesn't mean he isn't an expert schemer. And this situation positively howls with secret plans. All those factors add up to a single conclusion. The first step in connecting with Meimi is understanding why Father did this in the first place.

I turn to Cole. "You could have killed Meimi, or at least tried to. But you played possum against the wall, waiting for your chance. Then you sent Meimi to exile on Earth. That keeps her safe away from anyone on Umbra, including you. Why?"

Father sneers. "I needed to lock a door."

I turn over his response. "Meaning that to keep me and Meimi apart, an exile void was the only way to do it."

Cole shrugs. "The girl empowered you to steal my Crown Sentient. You don't think I'd allow that to ever happen again."

An idea sparks. Father brings up a good point. My new Crown Sentient could be very useful here. I picture them opening the exile void. Nothing happens. So I imagine more of them leaving Cole. Again, there's no response.

The emperor chuckles. "Checking if I'm right, are you? Like I said, you can't take in any more Crown Sentient. Not without the girl."

In reply, I quote one of the oldest sayings in Umbra.

"That horse won't run."

In other words, you're full of it.

"Not sure what you mean," says Cole.

"Crown Sentient are everything to you. I should be dead now, same as Meimi. And yet you choose an exile void to separate us. Again, I ask—why?"

Cole waves his hand in a casual motion. "Lost my temper." There's no real heat in his words, though. When Cole is actually angry, you can't miss it.

Lost his temper, my ass.

"It's like this," Cole continues. "The moment that girl took in my Crown Sentient, I knew she wasn't any more human than I am. She's Umbran and a conduit for my Crown Sentient. Can't allow that. Now she's gone forever. You need to accept things."

I narrow my eyes. "Out with it, Cole. You've got a plan. Just tell me what you want."

"If you insist." Cole slaps on a forced smile. "I'm a generous man. You can keep the Crown Sentient you just stole. All I ask is that you don't cause trouble. Forget about that girl."

Frustration heats my veins. "She has a name. Meimi. And she's my transcendent, not some girl."

"On that we agree, son. Miss Meimi is indeed a transcendent. But we differ on a single point." Father 's next two words that blow apart my world.

"She's mine."

Shock zings through my nervous system. "No."

Father's false smile stays firmly in place. "Took in my Crown Sentient, didn't she? What do you think that makes her?"

"Not. Yours."

"Being emperor ain't an easy job, son. Crown Sentient mess with your head." Father's eyes take on a strange gleam as he says the *mess with your head* part. "A transcendent will share my load. This is a gift from the omniverse—the very universe of parallel universes—and it's not meant for a weak boy without the sense of a newborn piglet."

A realization washes over me. "You didn't exile Meimi. You've put her in safe keeping until you can get to her properly."

Implications link through my brain, like so many dominos falling. Meimi would never agree to Cole's empress. My heart sinks. She never would have agreed to help Godwin, either. But Godwin wiped her memories.

"Why shouldn't I keep her safe?" asks Cole. "She's mine, ain't she? Now, do you agree with me on that, or must I get nasty?"

White hot rage heats my veins. Father wants to take Meimi as his empress. That's upsetting on so many levels, it's hard to keep track. Yet much as I want to throttle my Father, that won't help anything right now. Leaning into all my warrior training, I force my mind to calm.

And I round on Cole once more.

"Come on," I state. "The fact that you're not attacking me? You *know*

I'm Meimi's transcendent. And if I'm dead, I can't be used to control her. I can see it now... *Marry me or Thorne goes into prison.*"

A muscle ticks on Father's neck. "You should have lied. You should have said you'd be a good little prince."

"So I'm right." I lower my voice. "Tell me. How do you plan to get around the exile void? You need time to plan how you'll control Meimi. After that, you must have some way to break the exile void."

In reply, Cole swings his fist. Before today, this strike would have appeared whip-fast, too quick to catch. Now I can dissect every aspect of the emperor's punch, from the way his muscles ripple to the barely-detectable breeze as his arm closes in. One option for what to do next.

Use it to my advantage.

The emperor's fist draws closer. Once Cole's knuckles brush my fore-head, I crouch down, dodging the punch. Twisting my torso, I land a strike of my own, straight to Cole's chest.

Crack!

That sound is unmistakable. My hit snapped some ribs. The emperor clutches his torso, his gaze shifting between his injured chest and my raised fists. Little by little, Cole lifts his hand from his torso. His finger-tips glisten with the barest trace of blood.

"You caught me off guard there, boy." Cole eyes me from head to toe. "Whatever trick you're pulling, it won't last." He wipes his hand off on his thigh. "You're mine, too. Just like her."

The words ricochet through me in odd ways.

You're mine, too. Just like her.

Deep inside, some kind of switch flips on. Fresh energy streams through my body. The static hiss in my head turns deafening. Everything in the saloon transforms to stark shades of black and white. Even more connections form within my soul. Whatever is happening, my new Crown Sentient are at it again.

And I thought things were strange before.

Suddenly, my body alters. My shoulders grow broader. Each bone stretches. Muscles bulge. One moment, I'm the runt prince to a behe-moth emperor. The next thing I know, I stare at Cole dead on. We're the same size now. The Crown Sentient changed everything.

A realization appears. This will be more than one solid strike against Cole. For the first time in my life, we'll have a full and fair fight. One on one.

Yes.

"Don't underestimate me," snarls Cole. "I can also use you to control Meimi from the comfort of Umbra... or while trapped alone on a prison planet. Your choice."

"You must grab me first."

"I'm working on that." The emperor summons fresh Crown Sentient. The black particles swirl around his hands, only to solidify into the shape of a double barrel shotgun. My breath catches. The last time Cole made that particular weapon, I almost died.

Lifting my arm, I picture my own Crown Sentient encompassing my first. The dark particles instantly rise from my skin, creating a black glove around my hand. Slamming my arm forward, I aim straight for the barrel of Cole's gun. All the while, I focus on a single image: shattering the weapon.

What happens next only lasts a second. Still my mind soaks in everything as if it takes hours to complete. Inch by inch, my fist pushes forward as the shotgun disintegrates. Once I get within a breath of my father's actual hand, my knuckles strike onto what feels like actual metal. I pull away.

And I don't wait to see what Cole does next.

Jumping high, I lock my shins around Cole's neck. Twisting my body, I flip the emperor through the air.

Cole lands on his head with a smack. Floorboards shatter with the impact. Splinters and dust erupt into the air. Father hops back onto his feet, ready to return the strike with a kick of his own. His hit lands on my stomach. I stagger back from the force of the blow. Normally, I'd be winded from that strike. Not this time. Leaping forward, I slam my elbow into Cole's throat before kicking in the back of his knees.

My father lands on his spine with a thud. I stalk closer, ready for the knock-out.

Voices echo in from the street. I glance toward noise. That's all the distraction Father needs. A dagger of sentient forms in Cole's hand; he pummels me against the wall and presses the weapon against my throat. "Do you want an extra mouth?"

Quick as lightning, I summon a blade of my own and shove it against his kidneys. "Only if you'd like an open gut."

Father glances down. "It appears we're at an impasse. How about I give you some time to think? Remember, it's a good offer. Keep the Crown Sentient. Find yourself a new girl—there are plenty of princesses running around. Just give up on Miss Meimi. And one more thing. No matter what you do, say nothing of this to your mother."

I frown. "What?"

"Fooled you, don't she? I don't pretend anything. I'm a good man and a bad one, both rolled into the same patch of real estate. But Janais is something else. If you value Miss Meimi, you'll keep the fact she's Umbran a secret."

I tilt my head, trying to understand. Just when I thought I had it worked out, there's another twist. Outside, the rumble of voices echoing in from the street grows louder.

Slam!

The saloon door whips open. Mother enters.

And inside my soul, my life derails. As long as I can remember, I've worked to save the good man that is my father. Now a line has been crossed. Cole wants to make Meimi his empress. If the choice is between my family of origin and my future with Meimi, there really is no decision to make.

No one hurts Meimi, ever.

3 / MEIMI

Sweet mother of science, that did not just happen.

An exile void.

My parents were drift scientists. Growing up, Mom taught me all about exile voids. And what happened just now? That certainly looked like one.

Red nanoparticles? *Check.*

Transport between distant worlds? *Check again.*

Evil guy saying creepy stuff like, *enjoy your exile? Not required, but big ass check.*

Blinking hard, I scan my surroundings. Sure enough, I've returned to Earth. Specifically, I stand inside a metal container backstage at the so-called Liberation Celebration. Which isn't a bad thing, considering how it's the same spot where I left Earth for Umbra. And this particular celebration is why I wear a frilly pink dress in the first place.

I've come full circle.

So far, so good.

Stepping around in a slow circle, I examine the small metal room around me, scanning for a drift void back to Umbra. My heart sinks. All signs of sentient have vanished. Reaching into my soul, I search for the pulse of Thorne's inner life. I don't feel anything, but that doesn't mean he isn't alive. Anxiety tightens across my shoulders.

What's happening to Thorne now? What will Cole do to my transcendent?

I straighten my spine. *Nothing, that's what Cole will do. Because I'm getting back to Umbra.*

Together, Thorne and I can fight anything. And right now, the Emperor of the Omniverse is top of my list of Dickheads To Take Down.

There's just the little matter of how to make it happen.

Rubbing my neck, I consider my options. The easy answer to this problem comes in the form of my handy-dandy new Crown Sentient. I picture them opening the red exile void. Nothing happens.

So I do that about ten more times.

Same result.

Moving on.

For years, I built quantum gizmos to keep my family fed and well away from the government's notice. My handler, Fritz, always sent me the most impossible projects. For me, design begins when I list the pieces to bring together. Parts for a new creation spin through my head.

Dark matter monolith? *Tricky to find, but totally necessary.*

Wormhole detector? *Sure thing.*

Magnetic enhancer? *Buy in bulk.*

Beyond that, I stall out.

A jolt of worry zings up my back. There must be a way to do this; I just need to focus more.

Think, Meimi!

Something stirs inside my mind. My thoughts, which always fly pretty quickly, now zoom off on something close to light speed. Synapses fire in new ways. Odd connections form. Back at Umbra, I'd gotten a blazing headache while taking in Crown Sentient. Now that pain returns with a vengeance. Agony sears into my eye sockets.

And I start seeing things.

Namely, sentient cascade from the ceiling, the many black particles reminding me of a dark snowfall.

My heart sinks. Eye pain? Sentient snow? The stress must be taking over at last. After all, I just traveled through space. Not to mention how before that, I stopped an evil doctor from *cleansing* millions of my fellow humans. Either I'm finally having a breakdown or... that's really all I have.

The breakdown idea.

Which sucks because I'm stuck inside a box right now. Not the best place to start seeing stuff. What if I pass out? I could end up on *News Of The Bizarre* data feeds. I can see the headline now: *Supposed Genius Girl Locks Self In Box And Dies.*

Huh. I'd totally read that article.

The pain in my skull turns unbearable. Energy streams down my back, forcing my spine to arch and my gaze to lock onto the ceiling. My arms fall loose to my sides, palms forward. An eternity and a moment pass, all at once. More components fly through my mind, from star maps to software code. Pieces fall apart and realign. A plan begins to form. Nothing final yet, but it's a good start.

Little by little, the agony in my temples fades. At last, I can stare in directions other than up. Before me, the dark snowflakes cease to fall. Instead, they swirl and merge into a new shape. Surprisingly, it's familiar.

The Lacerator.

My mind continues to spin. More thoughts align. Before, I wasn't sure what was happening to me. Now, an answer appears.

Crown Sentient.

I focus on the Lacerator. "Am I changing?" I tap my head, just to make it clear where I think something has decided to make improvements.

The Lacerator nods.

"It's the Crown Sentient, isn't it?"

Another nod.

I hug my elbows. Not sure how I feel about some alien nanotech monkeying with my brain. Intellect is the only thing that's kept me alive for years. Still, I've never come up with plans this quickly before. If I'm able to build something to destroy that exile void, it will be thanks to my new Crown Sentient.

Meh. I'm keeping them.

The edges of the Lacerator's body stretch and flip, like image glitching on a data feed. I step closer.

"Are the Crown Sentient affecting you, too?"

The Lacerator nods once more.

The glitching turns more violent. One moment, I look upon my favorite dino monster. The next, the Lacerator has taken a new form entirely.

It's my sister Luci.

On reflex, I take a half-step backward. This isn't a solid statue kind of deal. The new figure is created from a swirl of particles. But the slim figure, long hair, and piercing gaze... that's all Luci.

Joy and rage churn through my nervous system. Growing up, Luci was my idol. I followed her in everything—doing all she asked and more— even if that meant working as a child in a garbage reclamation center. Over the last months, I've learned that my love for Luci was all one-sided. While I adored her, she hated me. Long story.

An electric sense of frustration curls over my skin. How can I still feel some affection for Luci? She betrayed me. Sold me out. Yet some part of me wishes to remain the little girl riding the hoverbus to garbage reclamation, proud to be seated next to her sophisticated older sister.

I focus on Sentient Luci. "Are you my sister?"

She shakes her head. That's a *no*.

"You're still Crown Sentient."

A nod. *Yes.*

"So you're here to..." I step near enough to carefully examine the particles. They're no longer pitch black, but bright blue. This particular shade of sentient see the past or future.

That narrows things down.

"You want to show me something about the past?" I ask.

Sentient Luci rolls her eyes. Another *no*.

"Are you here to warn me about the future?"

Sentient Luci nods.

"That's cool," I say.

Although to be honest, I could have used a warning like this a lot earlier. Luci already sold me out to Godwin's cleansing program, big time. Still, it's good to know Luci is still out there, scheming and causing trouble.

"What exactly should I worry about?" I ask.

In reply, the sentient take a new shape. It's a pair of life pods. One holds a man, the other contains a woman. For both people, their limbs are in disarray while their faces stay frozen in a scream.

When I speak, my voice comes out as a whisper. "They're dead." The sight bothers me much more than it should. My eyes prickle with held-in tears. "These people are important to my past or future."

There's no need for a reply. Deep in my heart, I already know this is the truth. I press my palms against my eyes. These are two random people who suffered an awful death. Yet for some reason, seeing them hurts me as badly as Luci's betrayal.

When I speak, my voice is a hoarse croak. "That's enough."

The scene bursts into a tornado-style whirl before reforming into a new figure. It's a stooped man with drooping jowls, a bulbous nose, and a perpetual smile. Although he's made from blue particles, there's no missing how this guy wears a tweed suit and matching fedora. I've seen this particular character many times on data feeds.

"You've taken the shape of Professor Conway, the Headmaster of ECHO Academy."

Sentient Conway grins. Another *yes*.

I shift my weight from foot to foot. "Before, I always wanted to go to ECHO Academy. It's the best high school for science."

Sentient Conway lifts his chin in agreement. He points to me and then the ground beside him. The meaning of the gesture is clear. *You belong with me at ECHO Academy.*

Prepare for disappointment, bud.

"Here's the deal," I state. "I just went to another planet and fought the Emperor of the Omniverse. Before that, I put together a team that stopped Doctor Godwin and his cleansing program. Going back to school now feels a little..." I bob my head, searching for the right words.

Sentient Conway points to the ground beside him again. It's clear that he doesn't care how I feel on this one. Conway thinks I belong at ECHO.

"I've got it," I continue. "It feels like trying to shove toothpaste back into a tube. I'm out of high school and not going back. What's there for me, anyway?"

In reply, Sentient Conway transforms into a new figure: a stick of a woman with thinning hair, intelligent eyes and lots of wrinkles. *Miss Edith*. Growing up, my mother spent a growing number of her days catatonic. When I'd go off on my gizmo projects, Miss Edith would stay to watch Mom.

I have a single question for the real Miss Edith. It's been burning away in my mind. Even though this isn't the same person, I can't help but try and satisfy my curiosity.

"Are you all right, Miss Edith?"

She frowns. This is a super-good replica of her. That particular look is Miss Edith's way of saying, *whatever do you mean?*

"Oh, I already checked to make sure you weren't hurt as part of Doctor Godwin's so-called cleansing. Are things still okay with you?"

She nods. *Yes.*

"Then why are you here and—" Before I can finish, a new sound rattles the air.

Boom!

The floor shakes from the force of an explosion. Like wind through autumn leaves, the sentient whirl out of a humanoid shape, becoming separate particles once more. One moment, the swarm is here. The next, they are gone. And I'm alone in a completely dark metal container.

Not good.

"I hereby announce the Fifth Age of Umbra, which shall be ruled by the Oxblood clan." - Empress Janais, author of *The Fifth Age of Umbra*

COLE'S WORDS still ricochet through my soul. Father thinks Meimi is his transcendent.

What a nightmare.

"Think on what I said," whispers Cole. "Say nothing to Janais."

Umbrans stream into the saloon. My eyes widen with surprise. This is the extended royal court. Like all Umbra, the nobles resemble groups from Earth's so-called Wild West. In reality, everything they wear—as well as this very saloon itself—are formed from high tech threads called filaments.

My mother, Janais, steps up. With her strong cheekbones, copper skin, and long neck, Janais is the very image of the word *queen*. Today Mother wears a simply white robe that cinches at her waist.

The way Janais crosses the room, it's not like her husband and son are pulling knives on each other. Mother focuses on Cole first.

"My love," Janais says smoothly. "The factions have arrived. Shall we join the conclave?"

What my father does next is a genuine surprise.

He gives up.

My father's dagger disappears from his hand. Cole raises his hands shoulder height, palms forward, in the universal symbol of surrender. Nothing remains except me, my knife and a chance to skewer the emperor's gut.

Mother rounds on me. With Father, Janais acted as if nothing were odd about his knife at my throat. With me, she takes a different approach. Her mouth thins to a worried line. "Do not do this, my son." She glances to the rest of the court.

Mother's logic is obvious. Everyone can sense that Father won't last much longer as emperor. The other two factions in Umbra—namely the Vingians and Komandir—are bulking up on sentient and warriors.

War is coming.

Today's conclave is to assure everyone of Father's sanity. Walking in on Cole about to skewer his son doesn't help things.

There may be a time to end my father's life, but it won't be in front of my family's enemies. I command my blade to vanish, then step away.

For his part, Cole gives Mother a sweet smile. For the first time, I see rage that boils behind that grin.

"However did you know I was here?" asks Cole.

"You're hard to miss, my love."

"So you say."

Father's logic here is obvious. Today's conclave is being held in order to prove the Father's mental strength. So Janais guides our enemies right into a room where Cole attacks his own son? It might be an odd coincidence.

Then again, it might not.

Cole rounds on the court. His demeanor transforms from false cheer to overwhelming charisma. The emperor steps about, glad handing delegates. The most important are the leaders of the two main factions, namely the Komandir and Vingians.

First, Father approaches Doc Pyotr, King of the Komandir. The guy reminds me of a music hall maestro—all tall and slick in his red striped suit. His top hat is surrounded by metal gears and lights, making the man super easy to pick out in a crowd.

Second, Father greets Locus, the leader of the Vingian faction. She's a nine-year-old girl with ebony skin, long braided hair and about a hundred previous Vingian rulers chatting away in her head. Vingians value learning, and their leader always gets previous minds loaded in her own. The thought makes me shiver.

As Father circulates, my thoughts return to Father's warning about Janais. How *did* Mother know where to find us, anyway? Any why did she walk in with the entire court without checking first?

I'd always seen Janais as a long-suffering saint who perseveres under Father's slowly-descending madness. Now a new idea worms into my consciousness.

Perhaps I can't totally trust her, either.

After finishing his greetings, Father strides over to Mother's side. "The conclave! Let's go."

Janais sets her hand on Father's forearm and she rounds on me. "Excuse us."

Together, they process out of the saloon. The court follows.

Soon it's just me, Justice and Slate.

And a lot of new questions.

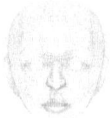

UGH. My ears still reverberate with the force of that mystery boom. If you're going to hear an explosion, the interior of a metal box is *not* the place to be.

I pause and wait. Will there be another explosion?

A minute passes.

Then two.

Silence.

I exhale. Whatever caused that explosion, it seems to be over now. Which means this is no time to lurk in the dark. Brushing my hands across the metal walls, I search for the exit latch.

Total flop.

I try to act cool. Who's afraid of being trapped inside a dark metal container? Answer: *me*. My palms turn slick with sweat.

At last, voices sound outside.

"Meimi?" That's Zoe who, along with her twin Chloe, are my best friends.

I exhale. "I'm in here. What was that boom?"

"No idea."

The container door swings open. Zoe stands before me, her right fist set on her hip in a way that says, *you've got to be kidding*. Even after all the excitement tonight, Chloe looks like a camera-ready movie star. Not a blonde hair stands out of place. Her make-up remains perfect. You have to admire that kind of skill.

"Thanks." I step out of the container and wince in the brighter light. "Now we need to talk about our next *heist for good*."

At this point, I'd love to chat about busting up the exile void, but I've learned that I can't jump into too much detail with Chloe and Zoe. At least, not right away.

"Another heist for good?" asks Zoe slowly. "We just did one and it didn't go too smoothly."

I shrug my shoulders in the universal gesture for *meh*. "It worked."

Zoe shakes her head. "Barely."

"Let me try again." I wanted to avoid this talk, but it looks like we have to have it now anyway. "Cole just opened an exile void."

Zoe frowns. "That sounds bad."

"It is. The thing seals all of Earth off from the planet Umbra."

"No." Zoe's big blue eyes widen. "Justice is in Umbra."

"Exactly." Justice is Thorne's older brother; Zoe is his transcendent. I guess it's rare for a transcendents to be Earther and Umbran, but it happened with me and Thorne, so why not Justice and Zoe?

Chloe jogs up. With each footfall, the pony tails on either side of her head bounce. She wears her classic overalls and a huge smile.

"Great work, guys." Chloe holds up her palms and waits. Zoe and I don't move. "You're leaving me hanging. Ouch."

Zoe turns to her sister. "Thorne's evil father just opened an exile void to separate Earth and Umbra. Permanently."

Chloe gasps. "But Slate is in Umbra."

I wince. "Sorry." Slate is Thorne's younger brother. He's Chloe's transcendent.

Such a disaster.

All the color drains from Chloe's face. "What'll we do?"

"I was just telling Zoe all about it," I reply. "We just need to figure out how to sidestep that exile void. It will be another heist for good."

Zoe taps her chin. "Is this a known thing... or are you making stuff up?"

"I've got to be honest. Everyone thinks that it's impossible to break apart an exile void."

The twins share a long look. "Huh," they say in unison. A long moment passes before my friends speak again. "We're in."

Some worry seeps off my shoulders. With Chloe and Zoe on board, things are looking up. I hitch my thumb toward the exit. "Let's get into the Simulacrum and run some ideas."

"Meimi," says Chloe.

I hold my hands up, palms forward. "Hey, I get that you have questions." Mostly because the twins always have questions. "But it *is* possible to tap into extra magnetic energy on the scale need. I did it once before with my mother."

"Meimi," warns Zoe.

My hands stay up. I've spent weeks in an underground bunker, rail-roading Chloe and Zoe into finishing the systems for today's heist. I know how to get them on board. "All we need to do is network some monoliths and—"

"Meimi!" cry the twins together.

Once Chloe and Zoe start talking in unison, my options get limited. "What is it?"

"President Hope is heading this way," says Zoe.

All the oxygen seems to get sucked out of my lungs. If Zoe had said that zombie Albert Einstein were dancing the cha cha nearby, I couldn't be more surprised. President Hope is on her way. As in, this woman leads the government.

Yipes.

"When visiting a parallel world, one must always be open to all possibilities." –
Beauregard the Great author of *Instructions for Visiting Parallel Worlds*

I DO A QUICK INVENTORY. Right now, I've got an empty saloon, me, and my brothers. Oh, and all those questions about Janais.

Beside me, Justice cuts a hefty figure in his long duster, heavy boots, and scarred face. Slate stands beside him. My younger brother is tall and sinewy with a long face and shoulder-length white hair. Like always, Slate wears a deep indigo jacket with a high collar and straight cut. Not for the first time, my brothers remind me of a cowboy and preacher from the Old West.

"What just happened to you, big guy?" asks Justice. "Got yourself a new hologram generator?"

I turn over this statement. *Hologram generator?* Then I realize what he means. Crown Sentient changed me during my last fight.

"Right," I state. "My height."

"Tall," declares Slate. My younger brother has a gift for both blue sentient and seeing the future. He's never been much of a chatterbox.

I picture my body returning to its regular proportions. It does so painlessly. If Justice wants to think that's hologram tech at work, I won't correct him.

"Better?" I ask.

"Familiar," announces Slate.

Raising my hand, I summon fresh sentient. "Look, guys. I need to get to Fort Derringer." Normally, it's both overkill and inaccurate to use a drift void to travel within the same planet. You rarely show up anywhere near your destination. But I have Crown Sentient now. Accuracy is more than possible.

"What worries you?" asks Justice.

I shake my head. "I've just got to leave. Cole is up to something, I need to find out what. Now."

"Wait," states Slate. Moving closer, my little brother pulls in his own sentient.

Damn. Those will monkey with mine.

With Slate's sentient interfering, I won't be able to finish my drift void. Not that I blame Slate for stepping in. Both of my brothers know I was weak with sentient. They worry.

That's over now that I've taken in Crown Sentient. And I could explain all this, but it would take far too much time. As would explaining how Father wants to make Meimi his transcendent.

Gah. Brothers.

"It's about Meimi," I say simply. Mentioning a transcendent is usually a great excuse for anything.

"Hey, we had a plan," counters Justice. "We must save Father. You can't go running off now. Father's at the conclave. That's where we need to be, too."

"You don't understand," I snarl. "Cole wants to *destroy* Meimi."

My brothers share a long look. Slate is first to speak. "Plan?"

"I must hit the viz dome in Fort Derringer." It's the most powerful of its kind on Umbra. "There I can check out different universes... and figure out how to stop Father."

"That's a predictable move," says Justice. "Cole will try to reach the viz dome first."

"Which is why I need to vamoose," I declare.

"Go." Slate lowers his hand. My brother's blue sentient disappear.

"We'll be right behind you," offers Justice.

They won't, not that I'll explain that now. Without Crown Sentient, my brothers won't arrive anywhere near Fort Derringer.

I push more sentient power into my own drift void. A heartbeat later, a full silver plate hovers in the air. Pulling back my arm, I punch through this round barrier. A gaping and jagged hole appears. After so many years, you'd think I'd get used to the sight.

Nope. It still stuns me.

A jagged round shape hovers in mid air. On one side, there's the saloon. Yet through the new opening, I see the busy streets of Fort

Derringer, the capital of Umbra. A single thought zings through my mind.

I must reach the viz dome before Cole.

Leaping out of the saloon, I land in Fort Derringer and take off at a run.

PRESIDENT HOPE IS on her way? Really?

Little by little, I force myself to turn around. Sure enough, President Hope strolls along the thin corridor that leads to our spot. She's all magnetic energy in heels and a skirt suit. Even though we've been working to help the president for weeks, it's not like I ever expected her to show up after all the drama ended.

The president pauses before us. She beams a smile at each of us in turn. It's a little overwhelming.

Actually, make that a *lot* overwhelming.

"I've been looking for you three," the president announces. "You just saved millions at the Liberation Celebration. Yet the event isn't over. I'd like you to join me onstage for the big finale."

Zoe, Chloe and I exchange worried looks. One advantage of being best friends; I know what we're all thinking here.

"It's like this," I say. "We're super honored to get invited onstage."

"Super," echoes Chloe.

"Honored," supplies Zoe.

"But..." I shrug. "We aren't exactly *get in front of the camera* girls. We're more *hang in the lab and change the world* types."

President Hope keeps right on beaming. "I thought you might say that, which is why I came here personally. Millions of citizens could have been executed just a few minutes ago. That didn't happen. The public must understand how that came to pass... or they'll make up their own reasons. Take my word for it. You control the narrative or it controls you."

Narrative shmarative.

I'm about to say that when an idea hits me. The Simulacrum. That's where we built our last plan.

"No can do." I gesture around me, Zoe and Chloe. "We need to get back to the Simulacrum."

"But you heard the explosion," says President Hope.

Unease creeps through me. "I did."

"Godwin had the Simulacrum booby-trapped," continues the president. "You three were supposed to go down in flames."

"Whoa," I exclaim. "That's annoying"

"What about the Tusk?" suggests Zoe. "It's a building on ECHO campus that studies magnetic fields. If we're going to find a way to break through a drift void, we'll need a serious magnetic boost."

I rub my neck and think this through. "Good thinking. After all, that's how Mom and I contacted Thorne in the first place. We leveraged a local magnetic storm to send a message to Umbra." I focus on President Hope. "We definitely need to hit the Tusk."

The president's grin fades a smidgeon. "The Tusk is firmly on ECHO Academy territory. The state co-funded the Simulacrum, but when it comes to the Tusk, I don't have jurisdiction. It's all Headmaster Conway. He's a little prickly."

"Not to us," asks Zoe. "We're students."

The president sniffs. "Let's just say Conway runs a tight ship. Getting you access would waste a lot of time my staff doesn't have."

"Some of the student crews have gear in their houses," offers Zoe.

President Hope rolls her eyes. "You do *not* want to get in the middle of that battle. There are bands of toddlers with better manners."

President Hope raises her hands, palms forward. "I'll do what I can about Tusk. You three have proved very useful. I don't want to lose you." Presses buttons on her watch.

Speaking of people who could have been killed tonight—outside of Miss Edith, anyway—the Hollow sashays up. Everything with this woman has a dancer's grace. The Hollow's skin is deep ebony, which contrasts with her short white hair. Silver implants gleam in her eyes and on her fingertips. She wears simple white trousers and a matching cotton tunic.

"You called?" asks the Hollow.

Unlike the president, the Hollow is someone we've spent tons of time with. I find myself inching closer to her. Safer territory.

"Can you get these three into the Tusk?" asks the president.

"They're already attending in the fall," answers the Hollow. "If Conway wants them in the Tusk, they can join a tour after their third year."

"Three years and a tour?" I shake my head. "We need access to the Tusk right away and *without* adult supervision."

"The headmaster will hate that." The Hollow lets out a low whistle. "Too bad Godwin is, you know..."

"In jail and his super-secret underground lab blown up?" I suggest.

The Hollow nods. "That."

A chill runs up my neck. "Fritz wasn't in the Simulacrum, was he?"

The Hollow's eyes light up before she speaks again. "Reviewing all data feeds. There were no living beings involved. Fritz has taken a trip around the world. A well-deserved vacation."

A low chant fills the air. "Hope! Hope! Hope!"

The Hollow turns to the president. "You must return to the stage, otherwise the crowd will tear the walls down." The Hollow turns to me. "Not to worry. We'll find a way to get you into the Tusk."

"That's good news," says the president. "Now, are you three going on stage?"

Zoe, Chloe and I share long looks followed by small nods.

"We'll go," I state.

Stepping between me and Zoe, President Hope wraps her arms about our shoulders. All of a sudden, I'm cocooned in her sphere of charisma. With that, President Hope marches us off.

What happens next is a blur. Zoe, Chloe and I stride out onstage to a roaring crowd. President Hope makes a nice speech about how our scientific minds saved everyone, yadda yadda. My friends and I huddle together and wave at appropriate moments.

All the while, I mentally list the equipment needed for what I've decided to call my Exile Void Annihilator. There were some good parts in the Simulacrum.

Before everything got blown up.

Godwin is such a tool.

The crowd cheers again, which snaps me out of my thoughts. I force another smile-n-wave combination.

At some point, we finally walk offstage. President Hope says we're all welcome to stay at the VIP Retreat, which is the ECHO Academy guest house for special visitors. Chloe and Zoe refuse, saying that they're staying with their mom. For my part, I promise to head over to the retreat. That seems to make President Hope happy.

There's no need for more chatter. Zoe, Chloe and I know what we want to do next. High-tail it away from the Liberation Celebration.

We've got a lot of work to do.

"Should sentient ever combine with filament, then anything might literally be possible." - Hammurabi the Seventh, author of *Law of Sentient*

I RACE DOWN the maze of streets that make up Fort Derringer. The buildings loom around me, from the grocer and sheriff to the music hall and dry goods store. The scent of fresh paint and old wood surrounds me. And there are people everywhere.

Speeding through the crowd, I make a straight line for the schoolhouse, which hides the entrance to Oxblood viz dome. As I move along, a small crowd closes in around me, blocking my path. A chorus of worried voices echo through the air.

"Prince Thorne, what are you doing about the factions?"

"War is coming!"

"My town was raided."

"Things have fallen apart since you left."

On reflex, I glance toward the route to the schoolhouse. Although I still need to beat Father to viz dome, my duty to my citizens remains.

When I speak, I take care to use an extra-calm tone. "Isn't there a conclave today?"

Once again, everyone starts talking at once.

"The emperor barely said a word before walking out."

"What a waste."

"The conclave dissolved within minutes."

"Now the emperor has locked himself in his forge."

At these words, a mixture of relief and anxiety churn through me. First, there's relief that Father's not in the viz dome. I can now research ways to protect Meimi. Second, I worry what Cole's doing into his forge. That's his workroom for new inventions. And according to the crowd, Cole ran right in there after ending the conclave early.

Firming up my stance, I clasp my hands behind my back. It's my standard leader pose. With that done, I launch into what I hope is a comforting speech. there's a lot about royal experience and how I'm taking a personal interest. Then I segue to my big finale.

"The royal family is in control," I state at the end. "Steps are being taken to calm the factions."

Relief washes over the faces around me. Folks disperse. I continue on my way to the schoolhouse, my thoughts churning over what just happened.

This isn't the first time the Vingian and Komandir factions have gotten restless. It always happens when Father seems especially unhinged. Everyone senses a change in leadership coming—and wants to be the next faction sitting on the throne.

Which explains why Father would want a new empress to show his head is cleared.

It's logical, it's just never going to happen.

Meimi is mine.

5AM

I stand before the Faraday Center for Magnetic Field Research. That's a mouthful. Everyone calls it the Tusk, mostly because that's how the building is shaped. It's a great glass tooth that towers over the city skyline.

Looking down, I inspect the semi-transparent ground that loops about the Tusk. Made from MonsterGlaz, it's clear enough to show the massive web of metal tubing that powers the Tusk under the earth. I kneel down for a better look at the magnetic reactor which serves at the beating heart of the Tusk.

Below me, a system of tubes and gears churn away, motions that remind me of a massive watch ticking. Using the mechanism, the Tusk yanks in millions of bits of magnetic info and dumps it all into a central database.

Rakki crawls up beside me. My little spider bot taps my arm with its pokey legs. I grin. This is Rakki's way of saying, *let's go already!*

Nodding, I press my shoulder satchel against my body, feeling the data pad inside. Between Rakki and this portable computer, I should be able to pull in enough info from the Tusk. My goal? Find a natural magnetic field that's powerful enough to smash through the exile void.

A shiver rolls across my shoulders. What's Cole doing to Thorne right now?

Shaking off the thought, I focus on the task at hand. Rising, I step closer to the Tusk. As I close in, I notice something unexpected. Posters have been set against the glass panels that line the first floor. I scan the text.

Bite The Cooks
Hobby Shop Kids Go Home
No Guards Allowed

I frown. The Cooks, Hobby Shop Kids and Guards are three of the best crews on campus. Cooks specialize in chemistry. Hobby Shop Kids are engineers. And the Guards are the finest drift scientists around.

Looks like President Hope was right; they don't get along and how.

Over the past months, I've been hyper focused on stopping the government's cleansing. Campus politics haven't interested me in the slightest.

Looks like ECHO Academy is one busy place.

Ah, well.

Time to break into the Tusk.

I step up to the entrance, which is a black metal access archway surrounded by a grid of red lights. *Pretty cool security.* Stepping around to the archway's base, I kneel and pop a small access panel. Taking a deep breath, I scan the campus around me.

No one's around. Perfect.

Pulling out my data pad, I use a ZoomWire to connect into the archway's inner systems. The Hollow got me this pad. She even added on a round sticker that says THE HOLLOW RULES.

Pulses of light move along the ZoomWire as my software infiltrates the arch. A moment later, a smooth computerized voice echoes nearby.

"Welcome, Meimi Archer. You are the first team member to arrive today."

The line of red lights around the arch flash to green. I grin.

Done, done and done.

After unplugging my gear, I step inside the Tusk. The first floor is an open space centered around a spine of glass elevators. After checking maps on my data pad, I take the lift to the top floor and walk out. What greets me is nothing less than the fancy-pants suite of the Tusk's Lead Researcher, Ms. Pattergee.

Pausing, I soak in the view. The office takes up the entire top level of the building. Nothing but glass all around and a great view of not only the ECHO campus, but of the Boston Dome beyond. I'd forgotten how the Tusk was the highest building in the city.

I press my palm against the glass window. Life is so different here under the dome. There's no decay. Holo-projectors create nothing but sunshine. Green lawns and perfect walkways abound. And, of course, everyone is carefully tracked and controlled.

I'll take living off grid any day.

Shaking my head, I get back to work. Right now, that means hacking into the lead researcher's desk, which is a long and slick number that looks as if it's made from black glass. Once again, I pry off a side panel and link a ZoomWire into my data pad. Clicks and beep sound. Another ZoomWire snakes out from the side of the desk, which I then plug into an access port under Rakki's head shield.

Or *try to,* anyway.

Rakki starts beep-booping and jumping about.

"Rakki," I say in the sing-song voice of moms everywhere. "Stop messing around."

My spider bot leaps over to the data pad under my arm. Using a pointy leg, Rakki punctures the HOLLOW RULES sticker on my data pad's casing.

Turns out, that sticker is no sticker.

The paper-thin circle tumbles off the data pad. The round sheet unfolds and expands, reminding me of some kind of whacked out origami. Soon what was once a sticker becomes a knee-high, walking robot with a bronze-colored body, round belly and what looks like an old fashioned camera lens for a face. Text scrolls across the round glass.

I'm Bobo, it reads. *A gift from the Hollow. She rules.*

I can't help but grin. "Do you take in data, Bobo?"

A panel on the bot's stomach pops open. Another data port is revealed. I grab a fresh ZoomWire from the main desk and hook it into Bobo as well as Rakki. White light pulses along both wires as my bots load up on magnetic storm information.

That's a pretty nice sight, right here.

Suddenly, an odd weight of weariness settles into my bones. Out of the corner of my eye, I catch a weird shadow by the elevator bank. My brows lift with interest. The last time this happened, the Lacerator appeared to me inside that metal container. I edge closer to the elevators.

"Lacerator?"

Something definitely shifts on the other side of the elevator column. As I close in, a sense of fear prickles across my skin. Not sure how I'm certain of this fact, but I know one thing.

This isn't the Lacerator.

A whir sounds as Bobo's head swivels in my direction. Fresh text flashes across his camera lens-style face. *Someone is coming,* it reads. *Look innocent.*

Dropping any thought of the menacing shadow, I race back to the desk. Moving swiftly, I pull out the ZoomWires from both Bobo and Rakki. My pulse speeds as I replace the desk's access panel.

Ding!

The elevator arrives. I tap Bobo's head. "Get back on the data pad."

Bobo just looks up at me.

Yipes.

I gesture between Bobo and the back of the data pad. "Become a sticker again," I whisper.

Fresh text rolls across Bobo's face. *The Hollow Rules.*

The elevator doors slide open. I hiss in a worried breath.

"Bobo," I warn.

Rakki crawls over to Bobo. Lifting one thin leg, my spider bot pokes Bobo and the stomach. The walking bot suddenly collapses back to a paper-thin disc. Exhaling, I slap the fake sticker onto the back of data pad once more.

At that moment, none other than Professor Conway marches into the room. I straighten my stance and smile. After all, this is my first official meeting with the Headmaster of ECHO Academy.

I wave. "Hello."

In reply, Conway just glares at me. His droopy jowls vibrate with held-in rage.

Huh. This ought to be interesting.

"In modern warfare, the main field of battle is the viz dome." - Wu Zhao Zetain, author of *The Art of Sentient War*

I STAND before a small structure with whitewashed boards.

The schoolhouse. I've arrived.

Shaking out my shoulders, I try to get my head into entering the viz dome. It's not easy. The recent encounter with my subjects reels through my thoughts.

My people are afraid.

No question why, either. Cole's visible weakness is getting the factions riled up again. Everyone senses a new emperor on the horizon, and they're gearing up for the battle.

A realization appears.

Meimi's now more than my transcendent. She can help my people as well. It was only with Meimi's help that I was able to safely take in Father's Crown Sentient. And if we do need a new emperor, then Meimi can be the key to that problem as well. She could drain Cole's Crown Sentient and name a new ruler.

It's a thought at that.

Still, thinking about how important Meimi is to Umbra doesn't bring her any closer.

Best to get moving.

After marching up a short flight of steps, I walk into the schoolhouse itself. Inside, I find a single room lined with six rows of benches. A central aisle cuts through the chamber, ending in a wooden desk. I stride to the opposite wall, which is a panel of whitewashed oak. As I close in, the wall shivers.

Then it transforms.

Before me, what had looked like oak changes into a sheet of glimmering filaments. The long threads part, revealing a black space beyond the wall. I step through and enter a massive and dark space.

The royal viz dome.

As always, the space that feels larger than a hover jet hangar. All around me threads of white light zoom and weave through the darkness. We call these reality bands, and they represent different timelines of parallel universes. The threads dart across the room in a great nest of interconnected worlds. Using this representation, the sentient show us which places need attention in order protect the overall omniverse.

I pull on the Crown Sentient within me and picture Meimi. "Help me," I command.

A new thread appears before me. It hovers at waist-height and pulses with red light. That's the sentient way of giving me a command.

Go here.

Stepping up, I grasp the band. A jolt of power whips through me, setting my hair on end.

One second, I wait inside a massive and darkened space. The next, I stand upon a sprawling desert formed of crimson sand. Heat sears into my skin. Two suns burn down from an impossibly blue sky. A white wall looms nearby, the surface engraved with the insignia for Vingian empire.

No wondering where I am.

The wall insignias are a total giveaway. This is sometime in the past, during the forth age of Umbra. That's when my mother's family, the Vingians, still ruled. Plus, the dual suns—combined with this particular shade of sand—means I've arrived in the red desert.

So I know my location and a general timeframe. Two questions remain.

First, precisely *when* have I arrived in history? The forth age of Umbra lasted for thousands of years.

Second, how does coming here help Meimi? For sentient, the past, present and future all exist at the same time. When the viz dome places me somewhere, it's because a chain reaction happened in one dimension that's effecting mine.

The infamous dimension drift.

All of which means that I need to fix something here, in this unique past, in order to help Meimi's future. Whatever needs repairing will shine with red light. The art form of these missions is determining what to fix before bad things happen, such as people dying. In some cases, whole universes can implode.

Bells ring out from beyond the white walls, breaking through my thoughts. Nearby, a swath of desert transforms. Just like the back wall of the schoolhouse, some of the sands change from granules into a section of long glimmering threads.

Filaments.

As the bells continue to toll, those long threads part. A great fissure opens in the desert floor. From the light of the dual suns, I spy a flight of stairs descending into the ground.

A long line of figures in white robes march up from the underground staircase. *Vingians.* This faction is dedicated to learning and science. The fact that a bunch of Vingian ascetics are marching up from the earth means that there's an underground laboratory nearby. These men and women dedicate their lives to research. The bells mark the end of the ascetics' day.

My body armor is made from sentient. Now I command those same particles to take the shape of white ascetic robes. While I'm at it, I make sure my hood hangs low over my face. No point advertising I'm a stranger.

As the Vingians march closer to the wall, the barrier shimmers. Additional threads form in the white stone. More filaments. The threads part, reminding me of curtains being drawn. Through this new entrance, I catch the pulse of red light.

That's my sign.

Whatever I need to do here, it lies beyond that white wall.

With slow steps, I take my place at the back of the line. As the ascetics approach the wall, a figure in black robes waits by the entryway. A guard. As each person reaches the wall, the same interchange happens. When it's my turn, I do the same as others.

"I am the Greeter," says the man in dark robes. "The Vingian Hermitage welcomes you home."

I bow my head. "Long live Emperor Valerik and Empress Alva." What I don't add are their unique titles for me.

Grandfather and Grandmother.

And the Vingian Hermitage? That's where my grandparents lived. No question about it. I've returned to the era when my grandparents ruled from a black tower within these walls—a place called the Devil's Fang. A young version of my mother Janais must be here as well.

Excitement sparks in my heart. Once I enter the Devil's Fang, what will I see?

Beside me, the greeter gasps. Turning, I follow his line of vision to the nearby desert floor. Once again, the sand transforms into long filaments that then open. Before, there was a set of white steps leading into the ground.

This time, it's a ramp.

The ground rumbles as warriors on horseback race up from the earth. *Komandir fighters.*

The women wear bright gowns with metal breastplates. The men don bright suits. All of them sport metal accessories, such as clockwork hats, hefty goggles and long swords.

As the warriors pound past the entrance gate, one cuts down the Greeter. Blood seeps out from his stomach to color the crimson sands an even deeper shade of red.

I instantly change my outfit once more. This time, I wear a black suit with a copper top hat.

And I follow the invading warriors.

The leader of the Komandir wears a silver star and golden suit. Even from a distance, I can read the name on that star.

Marshall Galveston.

What a surprise. To this very day, Umbran children still get told to obey their parents or *the Marshall will get them.*

The Marshall raises his voice. "Get the other Princesses." He gestures to a small group of riders nearby. "My elite warriors. Follow me. We're going after Janais."

It's an effort not to gasp. I've not just arrived when my grandparents are alive, but I'm at great fall of the Vingian empire. After the Marshall attacks the Devil's Fang, my father Cole rises from personal guard to actual emperor.

This is getting tricky.

I fall in line with Galveston's soldiers as they march through the streets of the Vingian Hermitage. We're headed straight to the Devil's Fang.

And my mother.

OLD JIGGLY-FACED CONWAY stands perfectly still. No talking, either. Just an old dude and his googly eyes staring dead on in my direction.

So I wave again.

Still no response. *Sheesh. What have I ever done to him?*

Oh, that's right. *I broke into his super-secret building. Heh heh.*

At last, Conway's face creases into a smile that does not go anywhere near his eyes. "Meimi Archer," he says in a crackly voice. "So nice to see you."

I shift my weight from foot to foot. "Uh, good to see you, too."

"How fortunate that we ran into each other here." That not-a-smile keeps avoiding his eyes.

"I guess." I wave Rakki forward. Since I programmed the bot's artificial intelligence, it already knows what I'm thinking.

If anything goes wrong, get ready to poke the old guy's eyes out.

Rakki moves to stand between me and Conway. My spider bot lifts its front two pincers in a decidedly menacing way. Ah, my sweet bot.

If Conway notices my aggressive bot, it doesn't affect his icky smile one bit. "Now we can talk."

"About what?"

"Umbra." Conway slips his wrinkly hands into the pockets of his tweed jacket. "I'll do you the honor of being honest. I'm planning a preventative invasion of the planet. I want your help."

"That is, uh, honest." *And insane.*

Conway purses his thin lips. "What do you say?"

"Since you were honest, I'll do the same."

"Please."

"Been here, done that, have the T-shirt. No more killing sprees for me, thank you very much."

"It doesn't have to involve much bloodshed."

I raise my pointer finger. "Can't help but notice how you say that it *doesn't have to* involve much bloodshed."

"You may have been on the data feeds with President Hope, but I'm still Headmaster of ECHO Academy. You'd do well to aid me."

Time to point out some reality.

"Look, Doc Godwin wanted my help in cleansing millions of people. That didn't work out so well for him."

"I am not Godwin."

So the fact that the bad doctor is rotting in jail doesn't really affect Conway. I decide on another approach. "Does President Hope know about this?"

"It's merely an experiment, so it falls firmly within my jurisdiction. ECHO Academy has nothing to do with President Hope."

"I'm pretty sure invading other planets are something she should know about."

"Invasion? Who said invasion?"

"You did. Like twelve seconds ago. *Preventative invasion* were your exact words." And yes, I make finger quotes when I say *preventative invasion.*

"Allow me to clarify." Conway rocks on his heels. "We simply wish to enter Umbra. Obviously, we'll need bring along Merciless warriors for protection. It's standard stuff, really. What do you say?"

"That doesn't sound like standard stuff to me."

"Is that your answer?"

"Allow *me* to clarify," I state. "The answer is no."

Conway blinks hard. Clearly, my response surprises him for some reason. "Why ever not?"

"Umbrans have tech you can't imagine. If you go there, you'll get slaughtered, even if you bring a ton of Merciless along."

"I've been studying Umbra for a long time," says Conway. "Trust me when I say, we Earthers have nothing to fear from those people."

"If you're so confident about invading Umbra, why do you need me? You have a whole school packed with smart kids who can help."

Conway rubs his hands together. "But you'd be the ideal spokesperson to the aliens."

Huh.

Saying I'm the ideal spokesperson? Total giveaway. No one in their right mind chucks a seventeen year old with limited social skills onto a hostile alien planet and thinks things will work out well. Unless, of course, the person in question already knows I'm dating their alien prince.

My stomach sinks. "What makes you think they'd listen to me?"

"You're such a charismatic figure. Last night, everyone loved when you went onstage with President Hope."

"Walking on stage and waving does not give me valid qualifications as an interplanetary diplomat."

A shift in the darkness catches my eye. My muscles turn weak as jelly. No question why, either. The shadow from before has returned.

"Excuse me," says Conway. "Is something fascinating happening by the elevator bank?"

I gesture toward the column of elevators. "Do you see anything there?"

Conway glances in that direction for all of one second. "Of course not."

"Right." I take a longer look. Whatever was lurking around, it's totally gone now. I'd go and investigate, but Conway must be dealt with first.

Conway takes off his glasses, whips out a handkerchief and wipes the lenses. "If you won't help me, then it places my visit to Umbra on hold. That's very upsetting."

"Boo hoo?"

"You wish to attend ECHO Academy? Forget it. You must remain in the VIP Retreat." He resets the glasses. "No classes for you."

Meh. Conway doesn't know I'd already decided that ECHO Academy isn't exactly my cup of tea. Not having to attend class actually frees me up.

Conway keeps glaring at me. It seems like the headmaster needs some kind of response, so I opt for a non-committal noise. "Humph."

That seems to satisfy Conway, so he continues. "Being buddies with President Hope means nothing here. Ruining my Umbra project does. You're getting a new guard. And *this one* will be more motivated."

That's a not-so-veiled dig at Thorne, who'd served as my last guard. "I don't know. My last guard was pretty talented. What do you know about him?"

Alarm flashes in Conway's eyes. He covers it quickly, but it's too late. I already know the truth.

Conway totally knows that Thorne is my alien boyfriend. That's why he thinks I'm his key to invading Umbra. Nice try.

The headmaster lifts his chin. "I refuse to chatter about security matters."

"Humph," I say again, mostly because he was the one who brought the topic up in the first place.

"Now you'll stay in the VIP Retreat and away from trouble. Am I clear?"

"Oh, I understand what you want."

I just won't do it, that's all.

"Vingian scholars once kept thousands of books on transcendence. Sadly, most of these have disappeared." – Empress Ophelia, author of *The Lost Book of Transcendence*

I FOLLOW the Marshall and his warriors through a warren of sandy roads. On either side of these streets stand small white-washed dwellings made from clay. Ascetics stand outside their homes in neat rows, their long white robes fluttering in the wind. Anxiety rolls off them in waves. Beyond the Greeter, no one has been killed yet.

Doesn't mean things will stay that way.

A tall Komandir warrior in a black fringed jacket steps along at our side, his silver star glimmering on his chest. "I'm Sheriff Jones. We're after the imperial family, not the Vingian people. Stay still and live."

It's a classic Komandir approach. As a rule, it works pretty well. After all, these are unarmed scholars, not trained warriors. The best move is for them to stand still and remain breathing.

Not everyone agrees, though.

The sheriff walks too close to one of the houses. Fast as a whip, an ascetic girl raises her arm. A simple dagger is gripped in her fist.

"Traitor!" she cries. "Long live the imperials!"

My heart sinks. This girl isn't much older than Meimi. Before the girl can lower her arm, the sheriff warrior raises his own long sword and slices right through the ascetic's torso. She falls over in two pieces, dead.

It's a shame to see any loss of life, but I've learned one thing in my missions to the past. Fix what's red, nothing else. Involving myself in other dramas can have unexpected consequences.

The rest of our journey is less eventful. Soon the Devil's Fang looms before us. It's a great black spike that juts up above the swath of small white homes. As our group approaches the tower's base, fresh filaments appear along the dark stone. Like the outer wall, these threads part, revealing a set of steps inside. Marshall and his cohorts speed up the staircase.

While the warriors race up, I notice a red glow emanating from the basement. My pulse speeds.

Another sign from the sentient.

Leaving the Marshall behind, I rush down the stairs, taking them three steps at a time. As I go lower, the red glow becomes brighter.

I'm on the right path.

The stairs end in black wall. As I move closer, the wall transforms from a slab of stone into a sheet of glimmering filaments. I step through. On the other side, I find myself in a dark tunnel. To move forward, I feel along the walls. Inching along seems to take forever. At last, the passageway ends in a space that feels as vast as the cosmos.

A viz dome.

Power hangs in the air, like the threat of lightning before a storm. The energy is so strong, I can feel it vibrating in my joints. No question why, either. The Vingian viz dome is supposed to be the most powerful of all time. Even in the utter darkness, there's no avoiding the sense of energy all around.

A point of light appears in the inky black. Once more, the sentient are lighting me the way. In this case, they have colored a nearby person in bright red, an effect that only I can see. I stare at the figure, trying to figure out who's here.

My eyes widen. It's Mother.

A young version of Janais sits huddled in the distance. For a moment, all I can do is soak in the sight of her. Janais appears around my age— eighteen—yet she still carries the stature and bearing of a leader. I move in nearer. Young Janais can't see me, but I crave a better look.

As I get closer, a weight of sorrow seeps into my bones. Young Janais' shoulders heave with sobs. She looks completely alone and afraid.

But she isn't. Not really.

One thing is certain. The sentient sent me here to help both Young Janais and Meimi. Now I must figure out how to get the job done.

A figure materializes behind Young Janais. *Strange.* I didn't know anyone could simply appear inside a viz dome, let alone make the dome surround them in a small pool of white light. I eye the newcomer carefully. He's a thin fellow in a fitted black suit and a bolero tie. With expert motions, he flips a deck of cards from one hand to the other in a never-ending arc.

"Greetings, Princess," he states. "I'm Lucky Uzziah Isles. Everyone calls me Lucky. I can fix anything."

Now, I've heard the story about my mother hiding from the Komandir on the day her family fell. I've even read books on the subject.

None of them mention a gangly guy doing card tricks.

"Go away." Young Janais tries to elbow Lucky in the shin. It doesn't work. Instead of prodding Lucky, her arm moves right through.

Young Janais gasps. "You're not solid?"

"No."

"Are you a sentient swarm?"

Lucky doesn't reply.

This flares my curiosity. I slip even closer. Lucky certainly doesn't look like a swarm. He appears as solid and full color as a regular person.

Young Janais elbows him again. Once more, her arm passes through. This time, I can clearly see particles erupt at the impact point. The colored bits swirl around the air before reforming into Lucky's shin.

"It's true," whispers Young Janais. "You *are* a sentient swarm."

Lucky holds his arms wide. "Correction. I'm *the* sentient swarm. Their king, you might say."

I frown. *That's news to me.* I'd never heard about the sentient having a ruler. Then again, sentient aren't necessarily a chatty bunch. Anything is possible.

"That doesn't make sense," counters Young Janais. "I'd have heard of you."

Lucky grins an over-wide smile. "I'm before and after. Above and below. You build viz domes. I am *the* viz dome."

Lucky's cards now fly into a great loop. I'd say that's magic, but if I look closely, I can see how each card is made from colored particles. The swirl of movement becomes a blur of speed. It's an unusual sight that quickly becomes familiar.

Lucky is opening a drift void.

A hole gets cut through thin air. On one side, there is the pure darkness of the viz dome. On the other side, I see a young version of my father. No scars mark Cole's face. There's also zero sign of unhinged rage —only a peaceful determination. And Cole wears an emperor's crown.

Young Janais slowly rises. "That's the captain of my father's guard." Her voice carries an unmistakable note of disbelief Clearly, Young Janais doesn't expect to see Cole anywhere near a crown.

Tilting my head, I think this through. Sure, I knew there was a time when my parents weren't emperor and empress. But I never knew my father served as my grandfather's personal bodyguard. The way Cole told the story, he was a rogue warrior who broke into the Devil's Fang and executed my grandfather.

Now it seems that the Komandir did the breaking in and killing. Meanwhile, Cole was protecting the emperor, not executing him. Unease thread through my soul.

What else has Father been lying to me about? How much of my life has been a fiction?

Young Janais frowns. "I don't understand. Why does Cole Oxblood wear a crown?" She says my father's name as if he's a breed of insect, rather than a future imperial.

"Simple," replies Lucky. "Cole Oxblood will be the next emperor."

Young Janais lifts her chin. "The Oxblood faction doesn't rule. They serve."

A sour taste creeps into my mouth. This isn't the first time I've heard Mother speak about Oxbloods like we were less than other factions. I figured that it was just a tough marriage making her bitter.

Perhaps I was wrong.

Lucky opens his arms wide. The image from the drift void closes. A heartbeat later, the hole in space returns to a swirl of cards before flying back into Lucky's open hands.

Huh. That's quite some trick.

"Nevertheless," says Lucky. "Cole Oxblood will be the next emperor. And *you* could be his empress."

Young Janais sniffs. "I'd never marry an Oxblood."

Shouts sound from outside the viz dome. "You know who that is?" asks Lucky.

Young Janais hugs her elbows. "The Komandir."

"If you don't like the future I show, then you can stay here and die. Or rush out and talk to the Komandir. Is that what you want?"

When Young Janais speaks, her voice quakes with fear. "No."

"Then try me. I could make you empress. What do you have to lose?"

Young Janais worries her lower lip with her teeth. After a long pause, she speaks once more. "Yes. Make me empress."

A sneaky gleam shines in Lucky's dark eyes. "Perfect."

Once again, Lucky's cards fly out from his palm. This time, they create a line that hovers high above our heads. The cards vanish, revealing what looks like a tear in the atmosphere. Tiny points of white light pour through this new fissure, each one landing directly on Lucky's palm. The sentient king clenches his fist; the dots of brightness turn into bits of darkness and dust that waft to floor.

"What was that?" asks Young Janais.

"I just erased Cole's transcendent from every reality," replies Lucky. "That way, you'll become his empress."

Young Janais frowns. "No viz dome can do that."

"This is more than just any viz dome. It's *the* viz dome. It's my place. My body and soul, as it were. You've no idea what it can do." Turning, Lucky stares directly at me. "Why the Vingian viz dome can even break an exile void."

My breath catches. Lucky was definitely speaking to me right then. What game are the sentient playing, exactly? Everyone knows that the Vingian viz dome was destroyed the same time that my parents were crowned. How could I use it to break an exile void?

Lucky gestures away from the viz dome entrance. "We need to step deeper into the shadows. They'll be here any moment."

"What?" asks Young Janais. "Who?"

"Others are coming. They can not see you." He flips cards in one hand. "Or stay where you are and die."

"They won't see us?"

"A Viz Dome is a great place to remain unseen." Lucky stares in my direction again. "Just move to the shadows."

Lucky and Janais step away. Soon, their figures are a small doll-like forms in the distance. Moments later, Emperor Valerik stumbles in while holding Empress Alva in his arms. Even in the dim light, I can see how both of their robes are soaked in blood.

Every cell in my body seems to freeze with shock. *My grandparents.* This is when they die.

Emperor Valerik lays his wife down on the floor of the viz dome. Neither of them notice that anyone else is nearby.

Blood lines the empress' mouth. "Where am I?"

The emperor brushes hair away from his wife's face. "We're in our Viz dome. It can fix all of this."

"Too late," whispers the empress. "Jewel... prophecy... safe."

"That's right."

Growing up, I lacked a lot in terms of sentient power. So I turned to books. My brothers say I have a scrap of history on hand for every occasion. In this instance, that works in my favor. I recall the gemstone prophecy. It was said that the very first emperor and empress of the forth dynasty saw a vision of the omniverse being destroyed. To avoid that fate, the imperials froze themselves in life pods, along with a powerful gemstone.

Is that the Jewel grandmother speaks about right now? It would certainly make sense.

The emperor lowers his head. "I address the sentient of the viz dome. Please, give me a way to save my wife and family." Threads of time appear above him. The emperor scans the many white lines, looking for the red color that means he can fix this.

Nothing crimson appears.

"Do you see a red thread?" asks the empress.

"No." The emperor slumps.

A familiar footfall sounds in the access hallway. Moments later, a young version of my father steps into the viz dome. Young Cole rounds on Valerik and Alva. "You must escape."

Valerik stares down at his bride. "Alva is gone." He touches the back of his head. When Valerik pulls his hand forward, it's covered in blood. "I'll follow her soon."

"You're in a viz dome," says Cole. "There must be some way to change this fate."

"I tried," says Valerik. "My time is done. If there's to be a new emperor, I want it to be you."

"No. I'm Oxblood. Warrior class. We serve the emperor; we don't become them. No one will accept me."

Valerik laughs, but there's no humor in it. "Then say you murdered me for being a tyrant. The factions will respect that. And you invented that new manacle cord."

"You mean the rope that combines sentient and filament?"

"Yes." Valerik smiles. It's a sad expression made worse by the fact that his teeth are stained with blood. "Hide the manacle cord generator off-world. Bring it out when the factions threaten to invade. Manacle cords block your enemy's sentient power. Combine them with your claim to have murdered me, and you'll solidify your rule."

This is another time-honored story getting blown apart. I thought my father hid his Crown Sentient off world. Or to be specific, with Meimi's parents. But it turns out Father probably lied about what he was leaving with them in order to hide his invention. It makes sense, it's just a lot to take in.

Cole sighs. "I'm no leader."

My heart cracks for my father. He didn't assassinate a cruel tyrant. He had to take down a friend.

"You can be," says Valerik. "Together with your transcendent, you can drain my powers. You'll see." The emperor raises his voice. "Sentient of the viz dome, show me Cole's transcendent."

Valerik looks up. Fresh threads appear above him. None are red.

The emperor shivers. "I'm sorry, Cole. It seems that you don't have a transcendent. That means you must kill me to take my Crown Sentient." Valerik pulls out a dagger and sets it against his throat. "Please."

Tears line my father's eyes. Little by little, Cole sets his own hands over Valerik's. Together, the two men move the blade in a swift and deadly motion. Valerik crumples over and ceases to breathe.

It is done.

My gaze locks onto Young Janais. She's been silent this entire time. Bile rises into my mouth. There was no mistaking the gleam in my mother's eyes when she said the words, *make me empress*. Then she watched her parents die—and my future father sacrifice himself—without offering a word of comfort. Who is this woman?

Particles rise up from both the emperor and empress. Crown Sentient. The tiny bits whirl around Cole, the many dark points turning into single a tornado of movement that reaches up into infinity.

I gasp. Cole is taking in Crown Sentient. This is the moment my father starts to disappear.

The particles return to Cole, where they transform into thousands of churning lines covering every inch of father's skin. With a small flash of light, the inky markings vanish into Cole's flesh. My father lies unconscious on the viz dome floor.

It is done.

Young Janais steps forward to kneel at father's side.

Cole's eyes flutter open. "Princess Janais."

"You had to kill my father and take his sentient."

"That's right." He winces. "These Crown Sentient hurt like hell."

"You'll get used to it."

"Valerik tried to find my transcendent."

"Do not worry. I'm your empress." She offers him a sweet smile. "And there's no such thing as transcendents."

"That's right." Father's eyes flutter shut.

Lucky steps forward. "What did I tell you? Now, you'll be empress. The cards are played out."

An ominous rumble shakes the floor beneath our feet. *Not liking this turn of events.*

"Ah, that reminds me," says Lucky. "We didn't talk about the subject of payment."

"What do you want?" asks Young Janais.

"My home," says Lucky. "Not that I don't trust you. But no, I don't trust you. Consider this viz dome out of commission."

The vibrations grow more violent. Red sand pours through the access passageway.

Young Janais gasps. "What?"

Lucky rolls his eyes. "I should think it's obvious. I'm burying every inch of the Devil's Fang under the red desert."

"No" cries Young Janais.

Lucky bows. "Farewell, empress. Better run or you'll be buried alive. One last word of advice." Here again, Lucky stares off in my direction. "The echo will be your downfall."

Echo? The term rattles through my mind. Echo is not a common word on Umbra. As a matter of fact, the only echo I know about is ECHO Academy on Earth. What is Lucky playing at this time?

There's no time to worry about Lucky and ECHO Academy. More sand pours through the entrance passage.

Young Janais shakes Cole. "Wake up! I can't rule without you!"

I circle about to the access passageway. At the same time, I change my outfit to the black robes of a Vingian guard. Once I'm at the spot where I could plausibly be entering the room, I race toward my parents. Now, both of them glow with red light.

Which means I must save my own parents from their doom. Talk about your crazy situations.

More sand pours into the viz dome. It quickly reaches up to my ankles. Waving, I close in on younger versions of my parents.

"I'll help you, princess."

Young Janais loops father's left arm over her shoulder. I take his right. Together, we march Cole out of the viz dome, up the steps and onto the red desert.

The moment my parents reach the crimson sands, their own bodies stop glowing with red light.

My mission is complete.

A hundred survivors mill about, watching in horror as the city slowly sinks into the sand. My parents step around the crowd, checking for injuries and lost friends.

For my part, I stand still and forgotten. Which is fine, considering how I just figured out something critical.

Minutes ago, Lucky said the Vingian viz dome can break an exile void. At the time, I thought the dome would soon be destroyed, along with the rest of my grandparents' home city.

But the Vingian capital wasn't destroyed. Lucky simply pulled it under the desert. It's my key to saving Meimi—the most powerful viz dome in Umbra still awaits me.

Now all I must do is find it.

6:13AM

Things are getting awkward between me and Professor Conway.

Again.

The headmaster keeps standing stone-still, his ice-blue eyes staring at me from under tufty brows. Guess he didn't like the whole *I'm ruining your plan to invade Umbra* conversation.

Tough.

I side step toward the elevator bank. Rakki follows. For once, my little spider bot doesn't beep or make click-clack noises as his metal legs hit the floor.

"Catch you later," I state.

Professor Conway's glare turns even more intense. It really feels like I'm supposed to say something else here.

I give him a half-hearted wave. "It was nice to meet you."

Thankfully, the elevator doors part and Professor Pattergee strides in. She wears a white lab coat with her black hair neatly wound into a bun at the base of her neck. Her eyes widen as she spots Professor Conway.

"Headmaster," she says. "I did not expect you."

Before my eyes, Conway transforms from a menacing glare monkey into a kindly old man. "Pattergee! I came by to check on your latest research."

"Happy to oblige." She steps up to her desk and begins pressing buttons on the slick black surface.

That's my cue.

Buh-bye.

I speed into the elevator and down to the main floor. The entrance hall now has a half dozen folks milling about in lab coats. Outside, a sanitation worker scrapes off the signs about the different student crews. A handful of kids meander across campus. It's all what I would expect.

Until I see something surprising.

Luci sits upon a nearby Plexiglas bench. This is shocking for two reasons. One, I thought it was very clear to Luci that I'd never wanted to see her again. And two, that Plexiglas bench wasn't there before. Who drops random benches off around campus?

Then again, these people throw out perfectly good clothes while the rest of the world picks through garbage. It may be something that happens at ECHO all the time.

Luci rises when I approach. "Hello, Meimi."

I stop. That vision from the Crown Sentient returns with a vengeance. Luci is up to something. Chances are, it's not super awesome for moi.

I grip my data pad against my chest. "Why are you here?"

She sits down onto the bench and pats the space beside her. The question is clear if unspoken. *Sit here?*

"I'm fine." That's my answer. *No.*

Luci slaps on a bright smile. "How did you like the Tusk?"

"Is that why you're here? Tusk research?"

"No, just wondering if you're doing all right. Have you met anyone interesting lately?"

As she speaks, Luci keeps glancing at the Tusk's top floor. Luci is many things. Master Of The Poker Face is not one of them. Clearly, she knows about my close encounter with Professor Conway. Which makes sense. If I were Professor Conway, I'd ask Luci to check in on me. Most people don't have such complex relationships with their own sister.

"Look," I begin. "You can tell Professor Conway I still won't help him. The Umbra is invasion is O-F-F."

A flash of rage shines in Luci's eyes. She hates being found out, especially when she considers herself as having been especially sneaky. The look is gone quickly, though.

A moment later, Luci is the perfect image of sad sisterhood. Her long blonde hair, big watery eyes and small pouty mouth all combine into the kind of artwork I'd find at the reclamation center. I'm talking images of big eyed children that are painted on velvet canvases. I suppose that look would have worked on me once.

Those days are gone.

I check my non-existent watch. "I'm running late. Do you need anything else?"

Luci sighs.. "This isn't easy for me."

"Then the faster you tell me, the more quickly it will all be over."

"I saw you on data feeds with President Hope. You know, after the Liberation Celebration." A single tear runs down her cheek. "You're all the family I have left."

"All the family," I repeat.

Luci never asks whether Mom is alive or dead. It's getting on my nerves. At this point, I'm not volunteering anything until she shows some interest.

"Please let me explain." Luci twists her fingers together in her lap. "What do you remember about father?"

"Nothing. Mom never kept pictures or talked about him."

"And you didn't ask?"

"I was busy. She was catatonic. We needed food. That pretty much took up my whole day."

"I don't mean to upset you. It's just that I've been thinking a lot about Father. Growing up, *he* was the one who resented you, not me."

Much as I hate to admit it, I'm very curious about what happened when I was little. Right before the Liberation Celebration, Luci announced I was adopted and she hated my guts.

Yeah, that was a fun sisterly moment.

Some small voice in the back of my head screams that I should walk away right now. Still, I can't help but stay. I really want to know more. So I sit beside her on the bench.

"Go on."

"Mother was the one who decided to adopt you. Dad just wasn't interested. And taking care of a newborn distracted Mom from her research. It ended up with them both getting fired from ECHO Academy. We moved out of the Boston Dome. Mom and Dad fought all the time." Luci sniffles.

That little voice in the back of my head pipes up again, saying I'm a total chump to keep listening to this sob story. Mostly because I might be feeling sorry for Luci just a little bit.

"Just wanted you to know that's how I got muddled. Dad said it was all your fault. I shouldn't have listened. "

I rise. This is the person who betrayed me more times than I can count. Two minutes on a random park bench can't make up for that. "Thank you for telling me."

"Besides, I know you're easily overwhelmed. I'll be here when you need me."

A little bubble of Luci-shaped hope had been growing inside my heart. Now it pops with a vengeance. Mostly because I notice how Luci uses the word *when*, not *if*. That's a very Luci thing to do. It's her way of saying, *you suck, Meimi Archer.*

When I next speak, my voice is ice. "I'm good."

"You don't understand. I'm your new guard. You're supposed to stay in your special chambers at the VIP Retreat. Josiah and I will check in on you. It will be just like old times."

"Huh." *And that's all I have to say about that.*

"Don't worry about whether I'll ever lose track of you. No one hides in the dome."

"Sure."

I've spent months under this dome. Does she really think I haven't hacked into its surveillance systems? Then again, Luci was never great at paying attention. Or doing anything, really. Which raises another question. With so many capable Merciless guards around, why would Conway trust her?

The ground beneath my feet vibrates. A rumble like thunder reverberates through the air. Sirens blare. Scientists in lab coats rush out of the building.

"Oh, no!" says Luci. I can't help but notice how un-surprised she looks here. "We better get down." She crouches behind the Plexiglas bench. I follow.

The earth heaves. MonsterGlaz around the Tusk cracks. Smoke billows up from the new fissures. Another quake hits, this one more violent than before.

Crash!

Glass shoots everywhere. The first floor windows of the Tusk explode.

"Oh, my! A bomb!" cries Luci. "The campus crews must be fighting again."

"I thought they fought like children, not terrorists."

"Whoever did this..." Luci inhales another dramatic sigh.

"My money is on you and Conway."

"Don't be silly. This explosion proves that it's too dangerous for you to be alone on campus. You can get—"

"Overwhelmed. We covered that already. And I guess Conway can blow up his own campus, but it seems like a huge waste."

"Oh, you." Luci giggles like I'm making a joke. Then she freezes. "Wow. Do you realize what just happened? I saved your life. Now you must know I'm on your side."

Rising, I stare at the ruined Tusk and stifle the urge to groan.

"What's wrong?" asks Luci.

"I still needed data from that place." I got a little with Rakki and Bobo, but it might not be enough to find a magnetic storm that can destroy an exile void. Not that I'm sharing any of this with Luci.

Luci's eyes widen. "I've got an idea. Why don't you talk to Professor Conway? I think he's working on some cool projects. I bet he'd love for you to join his team."

"I bet you're right."

Luci clasps her hands beneath her chin. "Should I tell him you're on board?"

Scrunching up my mouth, I debate about giving Luci a piece of my mind. Then I decide it's not worth it. After all, I did get some data out of the Tusk. Who knows? Maybe there's enough to locate the magnetic storm. Only one way to find out, and that's not by wasting more time chatting with Luci.

"Tell Conway I'm still not on board. And whatever game this is, play it with someone else."

Okay, maybe I did give Luci a little piece of my mind. Felt pretty good.

"What you're talking about?"

The sad thing is, Luci's probably telling the truth. Her level of internal insight is nil. "Look, I've got to go."

And in more ways than one.

With that, I turn and walk away.

Somehow, I doubt this is the last time I'll run across Luci.

"When returning from another universe, be prepared for your origin world to have changed in your absence." - Beauregard the Great, author of *Instructions for Visiting Parallel Worlds*

THERE'S enough chaos with a whole city sinking into the desert, so I don't need to worry about being subtle here.

Time to get home.

Summoning my sentient, I create a drift void back to my own reality. One second, I'm in the red desert of my family's past. The next moment, I step into an old-fashioned school house that's empty except for two people.

Slate and Justice.

And they do not look happy.

Justice saunters up the central aisle. His face is tight with a familiar combination of concern and anger. "You went into the viz dome solo. Have you lost your mind?"

One of Justice's main purposes in life is over-worrying about my welfare. Not that he doesn't have reason. Before today, most Umbran newborns wielded more sentient than me.

Huffing out a breath, I consider my options. I could take a big break here and explain everything to my brothers, or I could hustle out to the red desert and find the Devil's Fang solo. Besides, if my brothers know about the whole exile void situation, then they'll insist on helping. After all, Chloe and Zoe are their transcendents, too.

But I won't risk their lives. Meimi is my responsibility. Plus, I wield

Crown Sentient now. That means I'm in a much better position to fix things. Alone.

In the end, there's not much of a decision to make.

I gesture toward the exit doors. "I've got stuff to do. We can talk later."

Slate steps into my path, blocking my exit. My little brother lifts his palm. Blue sentient rise up from his skin in a small haze. No question what these are, either. *Knowledge sentient.* Slate's an expert in using them for intel of all kinds. For a moment, Slate's irises glow with blue light. When the brightness fades, my brother stares at me with wide eyes.

Now, I could step around Slate, but I won't. When he looks this way, he's seeing the future. Won't lie. I'm curious what he may have to say.

"I see plans within plans," whispers Slate. "Lies inside lies."

My brother isn't wrong. Between Cole and Janais, there's already a lot to track here. "What else do you see?"

My little brother shakes his head and blinks. I've seen his move before. A second later, his eyes return to normal. The vision is over.

"Crown Sentient." Slate's eyes widen. "You." My little brother is never a chatty guy, but he's always excellent at getting his point across.

I nod. "I took them in."

"Crown Sentient?" Justice fans himself with his Stetson. "Really?"

A half-smile rounds my lips. There's a parlor trick I pull on Justice from time to time. With my Crown Sentient, it'll be even more entertaining.

I imagine long swords stretching from my hands. Black particles rise from my arms and slide down. Long blades appear, although they are more extensions of my limbs than anything else.

Swiping my arm, I knock Justice's Stetson from his head. As the hat tumbles to the floor, I chop it up into tiny bits. To my brothers, this will appear as nothing more than a whirl of motion. The old Thorne would have struggled to cut the hat through once or twice. Now I can chop the item up into a hundred pieces, no problem. In other words, I'm moving the same way as our father.

Justice pats his bare head. "What in the ever loving—" He points to the floor. "That was my favorite hat."

"You always say that, and I always fix things."

After dismissing my swords, I raise my arm so my palm is parallel to the floor. Next I command my sentient to get to work. Black particles cascade from my palm to land onto the many pieces. The sentient reform Justice's Stetson back into a cowboy hat.

"There you go," I state.

Justice picks up Stetson and turns it over on his hands. "I see your speed, but I still don't get it."

"Meimi came to Umbra to help me fight Cole. With my transcendent nearby, the Crown Sentient just... moved over."

Justice frowns. "Is it permanent?"

I nod. "It is."

"So you've got Cole's Crown Sentient." Justice's tanned face goes pale with worry. "That's a death sentence."

"For who?" asks Slate.

My youngest brother has a gift for cutting right to the core of things. Slate refers to how Janais has wanted us to kill off father for years. With Crown Sentient, maybe I can get the job done. Unless Cole destroys me first.

"Father can *try* to kill me." I put extra emphasis on the word *try*. "I've got new skills."

"Cole has wielded Crown Sentient way longer than you," cautions Justice. "Maybe it's time we did the deed."

There's no need for him to explain in more detail. We all know what Justice is talking about here, mostly because it's the same thing Slate hinted at before. *Killing Father.*

I shake my head. "Even if we all wanted to do this—and I still think is a bad idea—then an assassination would take months to plan. I don't have that kind of time."

"For?" prompts Slate.

It's another good question. As of this very moment, Cole is no doubt hiding out in his forge, concocting some way to abduct my transcendent. I rub my neck in a nervous rhythm. Explaining all that is a time suck I can't afford.

"I simply must leave." Raising my hand, I summon a drift void. A silver plate of particles hands in the air nearby.

Once more, Slate creates a drift void of his own, ruining my own transport portal. If I depart now, I could end up inside a black hole.

"Tell," says Slate.

"No choice?" I ask.

Slate lifts his chin. "No. Brothers."

No question what Slate means here. Although we got shafted on the parental front, my siblings are simply the best. There's no way they'll let me leave without getting more of the story.

An idea appears. If I tell my brothers the barest facts, that might be enough to get me out of here without risking any more lives.

"There's no easy way to put this," I begin. "Cole sealed off Meimi with an exile void."

"An exile void?" echoes Justice. "You mean between Umbra and Earth?"

I nod. "I know this is hard."

Justice's hands ball into fists. "So Zoe's blocked off, too?"

"And Chloe?" adds Slate.

Poor guys. "That's right."

"Speak," demands Slate. It means he wants to know my plan.

I hitch my thumb toward the rear wall. "I saw some stuff back there in the viz dome. I think I know a way to shatter the exile void."

Thud!

The front doors of the schoolhouse slam open. One of Mother's courtiers steps in. "Janais would like to see you," she states.

Justice straightens his hat. "We'll go."

"Not all of you," corrects the courtier. "Just Thorne."

Memories of my conversation with Father churn through my head. Which parent can I trust?

I stare at the swirl of sentient particles that still hover by my palm. Sure, I could still leave for the red desert, but then Mother would know I've gone, as would the rest of the court. And information is power. If I can get a better read on Janais, that may help in my quest to reconnect with Meimi.

I lower my hand. The drift void vanishes.

"Lead the way," I tell the courtier.

It's time to find out what Mother knows.

I GET BACK to my room at the VIP Retreat. For some reason, the place is done up to look like something from ye olde America. There are pleated curtains, shiny wooden furniture and lots of portraits of George Washington. I'm not a fan, mostly because I suspect old Georgie boy is staring at me while I sleep.

Not sure what our country's real history is, but there are lots of cross-stitched pillows with quotes from Washington all around. There are three I find especially annoying.

We hold this truth to be self evident: those the state deems unworthy may not live.

Our opinion is your fact.

There must be no separation of power from the Authority.

Needless to say, I piled up all those pillows in the closet.

The one good thing about the room is that it holds a small desk with plenty of power outlets. My first task of the day is to fire up my data pad and do what I do best.

Hack into systems.

Soon I break into dome security and block any new tracking on yours truly.

Nyah nyah NYAH, Luci.

Next I set up an alert system to tell me where Luci and Josiah are at all times. *So easy.* I even launch my new system with the catchy name, *Guard This.*

Once I'm digitally cloaked, I plug in Rakki and Bobo so they can unload my stolen data from the Tusk. Before Professor Conway showed up, I could only download information about magnetic storms from the last six months or so. Mom and I originally contacted Thorne using one such event within that very window. If I can map back to that storm, I can figure out when the next one will happen. And with some extra magnetic power, I can squash Cole's exile void like an interstellar cockroach.

That's the idea anyway.

Better if I had more than six month's worth of data, but what I do have is a start. Plus, now that I have some of the Tusk's data, maybe I can find their offshore backups. That will get me all the info I want.

Hacking is so fun, I can't even.

After a few hours, I realize that the Tusk are a bunch of dumbasses who don't follow basic backup protocol. Scary how often this happens, but there you have it. That said, I do locate a ton of what I consider sketchy-pants magnetic data out there. Mostly, it's stuff uploaded from tinfoil hat conspiracy guys who are trying to track aliens from their mother's basement. Those foil dudes are actually on the right track in terms of alien life. It's just their approach is a little scattered.

Still, I download all the info I can find. If this works, I'll have to send notes to the tinfoil hat mothers that their kids aren't nuts. Maybe I'll even send them all free pizza.

I end up having caches of data all over the place. Now I need to crunch all that garbage down to a useful information nugget or two.

Which means more hacking into protected systems. This time, I'm searching for something with serious processing power. I start in the Boston Dome. There's nothing. Then I move onto the continent. Turns out, I uncover a system in Western mass that looks promising. Before I realize it's run by my old boss, the Scythe.

I've spent enough time kowtowing to that criminal. Plus, I know his stuff overheats easily. The guy's too cheap to buy a decent cooling system. No way am I uploading everything to lose it in a meltdown.

Moving on.

One by one, I hack into protected systems around the world. Nothing comes close. I have a vision for the kind of thing I need. Seems like my ideas are bigger than anybody's reality. At least, that's how the cookie crumbles so far.

Still, there has to be something.

I'm not giving up.

"Vingians led the forth age. Now, the Oxblood faction shall lead a new era." -
Empress Janais, author of *The Fifth Age of Umbra*

MINUTES LATER, I step into the Palace Hotel and march up the wide
central staircase to the second floor. From there, it's a short trip down a
longish hallway to room seventeen.

My mother's sanctuary.

I knock.

"Come in, Thorne."

Pressing the door open, I find a simple chamber made from what
looks like whitewashed clay. Like everything else here, this place is actually made from filaments. Scrolls, books and journals line the walls. It's a
perfect Vingian space.

Janais sits at a small table before a model of the Fort Derringer. As
Mother waves her hand over the miniature version of the city, the model
changes. Mostly, I notice what look like heavy pipes wind under the
streets.

I sit down across from Janais. "I hear Cole is in his forge."

"He's been in there since the conclave." She sighs. "Your father does
that sometimes. "

"When he wishes to keep things from you."

"Interesting as my marriage may be, I asked you here to discuss *your*
future."

I lean back in my chair. "Cole said something about me marrying an
Umbran Princess."

"You misunderstand me. I don't care who you marry. You must assume mantle as emperor."

I frown. "What about Justice or Slate?"

"They have more sentient, but I always knew you'd master yours to a greater level."

It's an effort not to frown. *That's an outright lie. Mom always said I was too weak to be emperor.*

Janais looks up from her model. "I never thought I'd see anyone beat Cole in battle. You could have skewered him."

"So now I must become emperor."

"Of course. That little victory is a sign from the omniverse."

I can't help but notice that Cole thought the omniverse was sending him signs, too. Interesting how these portents always align with someone getting what they want.

"This is beyond obvious," continues Janais. "You are to be the new emperor and I shall act as your co-regent. Your father is beyond help, Thorne. This is for the best."

Leaning forward, I examine the model more closely, mostly to break away from her direct gaze and buy some time to think.

What's the best way to keep Meimi safe?

Politics is something I can play, but I don't enjoy it. I'd rather stick an enemy through with a sword. It's the Oxblood side of my soul. We protect and fight with weapons, not words.

Although sometimes words are necessary.

Mother drums her fingers on the tabletop. "You've had enough time. It's not like Cole's insanity is something new. The question is, what will you do to protect the Umbran people?"

"What about finding my transcendent?"

Mother sniffs. "You mean that little human?"

"She has a name. Meimi Archer."

Mother leans forward. "You can't seriously care about her. Transcendents don't exist."

I work hard to keep my features blank. Based on this reaction, Father probably didn't tell other about Meimi being both Umbran and a true transcendent.

Sadly, all of this also means that Mother's been lying to me for years. She saw Lucky wipe out all Cole's transcendents. So Mother must suspect I actually do have a transcendent somewhere, and yet she's sending me off to insanity so she can keep the throne.

And Umbra doesn't even have therapists. This will take a while to heal.

I picture the girl hiding in the Vingian Viz Dome, afraid of being murdered by the Komandir. Mother now has a palace, husband and children. Yet part of her is still trapped in that darkness, willing to do anything to stay safe and in control.

"I'll say it one last time," says Janais. "You'll never find a transcendent. The cards are played out."

I nod, unable to form words. *The cards are played out.* That's what Lucky said to her so many years ago. Now Janais believes there is nothing to do but follow the fate she chooses.

And here I am, fighting both the future Janais laid out on that day... as well as the very forces of space-time. It strikes me that the truly crazy one might just be me.

"I know this is hard for you." Janais pats my hand. "Cole is getting worse. You're worried about finding the right way to end his misery. I told you before. I will plan everything. Just do as I say, and we'll all be safe. I'll send word. Until then, you're dismissed. "

Janais returns her focus to the tiny version of Fort Derringer. I even notice little versions of our family walking before the Palace Hotel where we live. It strikes me that she's much better at this game of people and places than I am. What makes me think I can I beat her?

My transcendent.

Meimi's beloved face appears in my mind. There's no way I can stand by and await orders while my girl is at risk from Cole. And I clearly can't count on Janais for help, or risk my brother's lives.

It all boils down to a single fact. I must leave Fort Derringer and find the Vingian viz dome. It's still buried under the red desert. If I can get in there, I can use it to contact Meimi.

I have to try.

After saying goodbye to Mother, I take off for an uncertain future.

GENTLE KNOCKING sounds at my door.

This is a bummer.

Why? I've spent tons of valuable time stealing all the best pillows and blankets from other rooms in the VIP Retreat. It took longer that I thought to arrange them into perfect nest on my mattress. Then it sucked up even more time to make a mini pillow-fort that holds my data pad at just the right angle.

No way am I ruining it all to answer the door.

I wait and listen. Maybe whoever it is will go away.

Knock, knock.

Nope, they aren't leaving.

"Meimi?" A pair of voices echoes into my room. They're speaking in unison, which means that this isn't someone wondering if I need more hand towels.

Zoe and Chloe are here.

I whip off my covers, slide away from my nest, and open the door. Sure enough, my friends stand in the outer hallway. I wave them inside, where we share hugs and smiles. Then I snuggle back into my bed nest.

"You won't believe what I'm working on," I announce. "I totally stole magnetic data from the Tusk."

Chloe plunks down onto the end of my mattress. She makes grabby hands for my data pad, so I toss it over. Chloe scrolls through my calcs and smiles. "There's a ton here."

Zoe looks over her sister's shoulder. "You've been a busy girl, Meimi."

I bob my brows. "You know it. What have you two been up to?"

"Meeting up with the Cooks crew," says Zoe. "They want me to join."

"The Hobby Shop Kids are recruiting me," adds Chloe.

I frown. "How did that go? Don't all the crews hate each other?"

"Abso-freaking-lutely," says Zoe. "I was warned that once we joined the Cooks, I couldn't hang out with outsiders any more."

"Same here," adds Chloe.

I gasp. "But you're twins."

"The kids are seriously twisted here," says Zoe. "They want me to create a mind control mist."

"But you *can* create a mind control mist," I counter.

"No kidding." Zoe rolls her eyes. "That was for *you*, though. I'm not helping the crews in their stupid war of booby traps and pranks."

Chloe nods. "It gets worse. The crews also ordered us to never even look at you again."

I grin. "So you came right here?"

"Duh," they say in unison.

Chloe starts typing away on the data pad. "There's some good stuff in here. With enough processing power, you might find a major magnetic storm."

"Right," I say. "That's the plan."

Chloe shakes the data pad. "This is so slow, it's annoying."

I roll my eyes. "Tell me about it. I need a better processor."

Chloe types away. "Based on this dataset and program, I've never seen a system strong enough to process all this."

"That's just the beginning of our problems," I announce. "Even if we find the storm, there are still major issues. Remember when I did this same storm-thing with my mother? Power surges basically blew up our lab."

"Right," agrees Zoe. "Then you flipped your house into two dimensional space time. Awkward."

I lean against my pillow pile. This is familiar territory. Zoe, Chloe and I talking through stuff. "I've been thinking. What if we surrounded some of the systems in coolant?"

"I can design some foams to help," says Zoe.

Chloe hands me back the data pad. "Do you sense him yet?"

No question who she means here. *Thorne.*

I shake my head. "Nothing since I left Umbra."

Zoe fixes me with a serious stare. "Do you think we'll see them again?"

"I hope so." A chill crawls up my back. In this moment, the possibility of seeing our transcendents again seems next to impossible. I shiver.

Still, sitting around doesn't bring our guys back.

I pull out another data pad and hand it to Zoe. "Let's plan."

Zoe gives me a sad smile and fires up the data pad. "You know what our mom always says."

I wink. "Remind me anyway."

Chloe and Zoe speak at the same time. "Hope and hard work, not mope and shirk."

So that's what we do.

"Sentient know all. See all. Do all." - Hammurabi the Seventh, author of *Law of Sentient*

AFTER LEAVING MOTHER'S SANCTUARY, I step out onto the second floor hallway of the Palace Hotel. For a long moment, I just stare at her door. A fissure of unease opens within me.

There's something I'm missing here, I know it.

Between the battle with Cole and journeying to Janais' past, there's been a lot of information in a very short time. Something is bound to have slipped past me. Normally, I wouldn't worry. Extra princes have the benefit of low expectations.

But now? Cole is after Meimi. I can't let anything slide.

Images from the past few days spin through my mind. There's the strange model city in Mother's sanctuary... Cole declaring that my girl is his transcendent... And Mother leaning forward to state, *you mean that little human? You can't possibly care about her.*

Turning away, I step through the Palace Hotel. My footsteps echo in strange ways as I walk down the main staircase. Usually, there are courtiers and palace workers milling about.

Not today.

The first floor is all faded velvet furniture, gleaming wood floors and silence. Inside me, fresh lines of unease wind through my chest. I pull open the front door and step out onto the dusty street beyond. The city looks deserted.

I grew up in Fort Derringer. I've never seen the streets empty, day or night. The intense quiet makes my ears ring. Every nerve in my body goes on alert. I may not be an expert at wordplay, but I do know quite a bit about battle.

Something hunts me.

A rumble sounds, deep as thunder. The ground shimmies. An image appears in my mind: Janais' model of Fort Derringer. Heavy pipes had been added under the streets. I'd assumed they were mainline filaments added to reinforce the connected web of threads that make up the city.

My eyes widen. There's another kind of filament that's extra heavy.

Oh, no.

The ground before me vibrates and breaks. Black filaments burst through. These are twisted cords of smaller treads held together by black sentient.

Manacle cords—my father's invention.

These block sentient power and make it easy to lock up Umbrans. And although he created them, even Cole can't break through manacle cords. At least, not right away.

Alarm rattles through my nervous system. These manacle cords were set here to entrap me. It's obvious who set them in place, too.

My mother.

I could run.

I won't.

If I were going to flinch or hide, it would have been one of the many times father was trying to beat me to death, not when some manacle cords grab me.

I firm up my stance and hold my chin high. The heavy cords whip up my arms and ankles, locking me in place. To test things out, I try to access my sentient power.

It doesn't work. At all.

Although my pulse speeds, I work hard to look calm. At this point, it's all I can do.

Janais steps into my line of vision. Pausing, she folds her arms over her chest. "You should have been honest with me."

"About what?"

"Meimi."

"I told you about her."

"Lies! I know ECHO academy will destroy me. It took me ages to pinpoint the precise person and place."

I remember Lucky's words back in the viz dome.

The echo will be your downfall.

At the time, I'd hoped it meant something other than ECHO Academy. Looks like I was wrong.

Janais' body shakes with rage. "I know your human is now attending ECHO Academy. She's a threat to me and you know it... or you *should* have known. Either way, you are blinded by your own stupidity. That makes you a liability, my son." Her gaze snaps over to the forge, which is a small wooden building halfway down the street. Father still hasn't set foot outside it.

Realization washes over me. "This has nothing to do with Meimi. Not really."

Janais stakes a half-step backward. "I don't know what you mean." She looks over to the forge once more.

Slate's words echo in my mind.

Plans within plans; lies inside lies.

Here we go again. More double-talk and secret schemes.

I focus on Mother. "Father said something to you, didn't he? Whatever it was, you know he wants to protect me. I'm valuable to him, so you wish to put me to under lock and key. It gives you leverage."

Janais' mouth hangs open for a long moment. It's about as close to a confirmation as I'll ever get. "I don't want leverage. I pray for wise sons who'll protect me. Isn't that right?"

At this point, Slate and Justice, step into view.

"Yes, Mother," they say in unison.

The sight makes my chest tighten. A betrayal from Janais is something I expected. But having Justice and Slate show up? I didn't see that coming.

And it hurts like hell.

Plans within plans; lies inside lies.

"You're such a disappointment," says Janais.

The hefty filaments drag me down into the earth. The last thing I spy are the unreadable looks on my brothers' faces as I'm dragged underground.

I can't believe it.

It's eight o'clock and I'm back at the Golden Pantheon building and wearing yet another fancy dress. I'm even sitting at the exact same spot where I did at the last Liberation Celebration. But that was so three weeks ago. Tonight's event is very different.

On the main stage, the wall of monitors now reads, *Welcome ECHO Academy, Senior Class!* Everyone's here with their parents and loved ones. I have Chloe, Zoe, and their mother at my table. Since they're both dressed up in blue gowns, the twins are hard to tell apart. You have to look carefully to see the grease stains still on Chloe's neck. That's always a dead giveaway.

Beside the twins, their Mom looks like an older version of her daughters, only with gray hair, more laugh lines, and a proud gleam in her eyes.

I slap on my own version of a happy look, but it isn't easy. I miss Thorne something awful.

Lights flash across the main stage. The monitors change to read, *Professor Conway, Headmaster of ECHO Academy*. A stooped man with a jumble of white hair ambles onstage.

Welcome creep.

Across the table, Chloe and Zoe watch the stage with rapt attention. I don't blame them. Attending ECHO Academy is a true honor for anyone. Just not me. I'm here as their guest, which is perfectly fine with yours truly.

Conway starts blabbing about how amazing it will be for everyone to attend *his* school. I eye my satchel in its hiding spot under the table.

Inside, there's my data pad as well as Rakki. Would it be rude to start doing a little work?

Probably.

But would it be *really* rude?

I pull out my data pad, set it on my lap, and get to it. All the while, the ceremony continues. President Hope comes out. A choir sings some tunes. More professors get up and talk. I'm fishing around my satchel for Rakki when none other than Porter Saint-Clare approaches our table. In the world of science, Porter is the closest we have to boy band material.

Let the record show that I do not *squee*.

Porter stares right at me. He looks just like he does in the data feeds, too: wavy black hair, sharp jawline, and bright blue eyes. He's a little shorter in real life than I'd expect, but what he lacks in vertical skills he's more than made up for in his outfit. Tonight, Porter wears a white jacket with black trim and one of those straw hats that people wear in old Earth movie stills, yet no one can get away with in real life.

Unless you're Porter Saint-Clare.

"Hello, everyone," he says with a million-watt smile. I notice absently that he has dimples and yet they do nothing for me. Interesting. "I'm Porter Saint-Clare."

"We know who you are," says Mrs. Fine. "Chloe and Zoe are always reading about you in the data feeds."

My best friends turn gray. Leave it to a mom to say something supremely humiliating. They must get classes in that along with what kind of diaper wipes to choose.

Porter slips onto the chair beside me. "I wanted to introduce myself," he begins. "And to say how impressed I was with the way you saved my aunt's life. That means a lot."

Chloe, Zoe, and I give our standard replies. It was our duty. Happy to help. You're welcome. It's the kind of garbage we've been spewing out to data feeds and reporters for weeks.

"So." Porter rubs his palms together. "What do you plan to do when you get to ECHO?"

I frown. "I don't know. Go to class?"

I'm not advertising how I've been essentially kicked out, mostly because it starts a lot of awkward questions. Only Chloe and Zoe know the truth.

"No," counters Porter. "For your senior project. Everyone has one."

"Oh, that." My gaze locks with Zoe and Chloe. "My friends and I want to build something called an Exile Void Annihilator."

"Wow." Porter has a way of looking at you like whatever you said is the most interesting thing ever. We make some small talk about our senior project.

That's when it hits me. A while back, Chloe mentioned some of the crews have tech.

"You're in the Guards," I begin.

"We're the best on campus."

"Oh. I was wondering. Do you have lab equipment at your house?"

"You mean, the Castle?"

I stifle the urge to roll my eyes. *Of course, they call it the castle.*

"I need something with mega processing power," I state. "I haven't been able to find anything yet, but I know that if you really want to avoid hackers, then you just keep your junk unplugged. Maybe you have some powered-down stuff that could be useful?"

A sneaky gleam shines in Porter's eyes. "Something like that would be illegal."

Yes. He so has the goods.

"I'd love to come by your amazing Castle place for a tour."

"Absolutely. I figured you'd want to, what with your history and all."

"You mean what happened at the Liberation Celebration?"

"No, your parents were Guards."

The room seems to freeze. My heart beats so hard, the sound of my own pulse rushes in my head. My adopted parents were guards. I didn't know that. Although I guess I should have suspected it.

Porter lowers his voice to a conspiratorial air. "We have a discarded processing station from the old Archer Omni lab." He bobs his brows. "And we do keep it unplugged."

A chill crawls up my neck. "You're kidding."

"Not even," says Porter. "Folks knew how to do things in the old days."

I exhale. "Wow. That would really help me out."

"Just come solo, you know how it is."

"Not really."

Porter scans the table. "Chloe is joining the Hobby Shop Kids; Zoe's being courted by the Cooks. We don't get along with those crews."

"It can't be that bad," I counter.

"Oh, you have no idea."

And the way Porter says those five words? I'm starting to believe him.

"When it comes to war, never forget the power of imprisonment." - Wu Zhao Zetain, author of *The Art of Sentient War*

MOTHER'S MANACLE cords drag me through the ground before spitting me out into a darkened prison on the outskirts of Fort Derringer.

That was two weeks ago.

I've been in this same cell ever since.

Thank you, Mom.

Once again, I scan my overly-familiar surroundings. A small window-hole affords the only light. There's no visible way in or out.

Nearby, a small square of dirt floor transforms into filaments. Those threads part, revealing a small metal tray that holds a large bowl of slop and a small jug of water. Stuff like this shows up at regular intervals. Based on the food and shifting sunlight, I figure that I've been here for seventeen days.

My appetite is nil. Still, I force myself to down the water and force in a few bites of goop. With that, I begin my daily ritual. Before I'd been imprisoned, it felt as if my head overflowed with too many facts to sort through properly. Now I spend every day sorting through all the questions in my mind.

What is Cole making in his forge?

Why is the gemstone prophecy important?

How much will Janais do to retain her crown?

And most importantly, where can I find the Devil's Fang?

I rest my arms on my bent knees, close my eyes, and concentrate. According to history, the Devil's Fang was located somewhere in the red desert. All records of its precise location are gone. Even worse, the red desert takes up a huge swath of Umbra's surface.

Not sure how long I sit and think. At some point, sunlight gets swapped out for moonbeams. I notice two more untouched metal trays of different colored-gunk nearby. Facts continue to swirl in new ways until a new memory appears.

A seven-year-old version of me slips into my mother's sanctuary. Janais isn't there, which is exactly what I had hoped for.

Tiptoeing across the room, I scan the journals on Mother's shelves. On each spine there's the image of another flower. After pulling down one of the books, I flip through the pages. Numbers cover the sheets. It's a cipher, and I want to crack the code. Some of the numbers are in Mother's loopy style, while others are crisp and vertical. Clearly, two people have been writing in these journals.

That's when it hits me.

Each journal has a cover with a long floral name written in English, not numbers. As a child I memorized those letters. Now they appear in my head once more.

Rosa moschata, the musk rose.

Meimifloria, the drift rose.

Rosa Luciae, the memorial rose.

Those last two? Those are not only actual Earth flowers. They're also the full names of Meimi and her sister. More information aligns. The extra sets of handwriting in those journals—perhaps one of Meimi's parents wrote in them.

I'd always known that Rose and Truman Archer had helped out Father. But I never wondered how they'd all met in the first place.

Now, the answer is obvious.

Based on Lucky's suggestion, Mother found ECHO Academy. It must have been Janais who connected Rose and Truman with my father. And once the favor for Cole was done, Janais secretly stayed in touch.

Meimi's parents now live in an isolated corner of Umbra that sits right beside the red desert. Perhaps Meimi's parents know something about the Devil's Fang. They are scientists, after all. Who knows what they've picked up over the years?

Suddenly, the wall behind my back shakes. Rumbles sound. Cracks appear. Shouting echoes in from the street beyond. I hop to my feet, summoning my sentient to take the shape of body armor. A single question rattles through my head.

Has the faction war finally broken out?

Whoa.

Am I really leaving a party with none other than Porter Saint Clare?

This guy has been named World's Hottest Teenager for two years in a row. I'm not proud of this, but I've read the articles. Porter is nineteen, charming, smart, and well dressed. Paparazzi follow this guy around. Leaving a welcome dinner with Porter will definitely cause some whispers. Everyone will assume I'm just another float in his Bimbo Parade.

But taking off with him will also mean I get access to an actual supercomputer from my parents' old lab.

No question what to do, really.

I turn to Chloe and Zoe. "Porter and I are out of here." My friends handle this turn of events in classic fashion.

Zoe gasps.

Chloe grins.

Inside, I squirm. *Here it comes.* Like everyone else, my friends will assume I'm another wannabe Porter Girl. I lower my voice to a tone that only Zoe and Chloe can hear. "Look, before you get any ideas—"

"Did you find a processor?" asks Chloe.

"Tell me it's a supercomputer," adds Zoe.

I frown. "Wait a second. You're not even considering the fact that we're hooking up?"

Zoe lowers her voice to a hiss. "You and that guy? He's not your type."

"Why not?" I ask. "He's famous and hot."

Porter leans in. "Are you talking about me again?" He winks.

Zoe purses her lips in a way that says, *and this is what I'm talking about. She's right, obviously.* So I cut to the chase. "Zoe guessed it."

"Knew it." Zoe beams. She mouths a single word to Chloe. *Super-computer.*

"Want to check out the tech now?" asks Porter. "No better time."

"What makes you think I'd be ready to go right this second?" I ask.

"You're wearing a formal gown with a satchel large enough to carry both a data pad and a small bot, if I'm not mistaken."

Which is true. I shrug. "You never know when you'll have a few minutes to do science stuff."

"Plus, it's easier to sneak in while the welcome dinner is still rolling. All my crew are here. The Castle will be empty."

"In that case, let's go."

Porter rises and offers me his arm. I hitch my satchel over my shoulder in a way that says, *welcome to the friend zone.*

As we step across the auditorium floor, it feels like all eyes are glued in our direction. A few flashes go off as folks take pictures.

Awkward.

The good news is that no one follows us as Porter and I make our way across campus. Soon we reach a tall white building fronted by heavy columns. The Castle. Porter leads us around back, where I find a set of double-doors set into the ground. Porter types some codes into the access panel before pulling the entrance open.

"After you," he offers.

A thought hits me. I'm slinking into a random basement with a guy I barely know. Then again, I have Rakki in my bag and a good aim when I kick for the balls. Plus there's also a supercomputer to be toyed with.

I'm going in.

Stepping through the doors, I march down some stairs and into the basement below. A single old-fashioned bulb hangs from the ceiling, casting the place in a halo of sickly yellow light. Metal shelves overflow with papers. Boxes stand in random piles on the floor. Random faded photos and magazine clippings are taped to the cement walls.

Not really what I pictured when Porter said secret laboratory.

I sniff. "This is kind of a mess."

"How do you think we hid the supercomputer?"

I nod, impressed. "That's good thinking."

Porter pulls aside a large cardboard box, revealing a square worksta-tion underneath. It's a block of a computing equipment topped by a monitor and keyboard. The logos of the Old Americas are slapped on the side of everything.

What a beauty.

I'd seen pieces of this equipment back in my mother's old lab. Still, that stuff was chipped and filthy—a mishmash of parts from multiple sources. But this thing? It looks manufactured yesterday. I kneel beside the main server and pop off an access panel. Everything inside is pristine. I pull out a ZoomWire and open my bag. Rakki leaps out.

Porter steps up. "Is that a spider bot?"

Does Mister Teen Idol sound a little awestruck by my sweet bot? Yes, yes he does.

And do I love that? Oh, you know it.

"Yup. It's an old model. I enhanced the AI." For my encore performance, I pull out my data pad. After Rakki pokes the Hollow's sticker, Bobo appears.

Porter outright gasps. "Whoa. Where did you get that?"

"It's classified." I wink.

Pulling out another ZoomWire, I pop the first into Rakki and the second into Bobo. From there, I use my data pad to upload info from Tusk, all while accessing the processing energy of my parents' old workstation. The system flies through the data.

Ah, computing power.

I get to work on some hacks while Porter watches over my shoulder. "What are you doing now?"

"Writing a quick program to cross reference data and look for a pattern of historical magnetic anomalies."

"Cool."

My screen flashes. "And there we have it—a prediction for the next major magnetic storm." I click a few keys. "The Andromeda Anomaly is due soon."

"Are you sure? Those storms are totally random."

"You've run across them before?"

"Oh, yeah. Campus equipment is pretty sensitive, so those anomalies can shut everything down. And you're certain that you can predict the next one?"

"It hits in twenty four hours and some change. I need to harness the storm's power for something big."

"Looking for an assistant?" All signs of Mister Snarky are gone. Porter is all Science Guy right now. I like this version much better.

"As a matter of fact, I do. To get this particular gig done, I'll need help from the three big crews: Cooks, Guards and the Hobby Ship Kids."

Porter rolls his eyes. "You're dreaming. We hate each other. As in loathe."

"I've been there before. You saw how my team stopped the cleansing. Let's just say we didn't start off all lovey-dovey, worky-worky."

Porter sniffs. "Even if you can get everyone to team up—and I don't think you can—then you still have bigger problems. Equipment. This isn't something you can do in this basement. You'll need a specialty lab."

I glance around. Porter has a point. This place is a total hole.

My eye catches on one of the pictures taped to the wall. It's a laboratory with a sign hanging from the ceiling—Archer Omni. My breath catches.

That's my parents' old lab.

With hesitant steps, I move closer to the picture. I gingerly brush my fingertips over the glossy surface.

Porter steps up beside me. "You haven't seen that picture before?"

"No, my mother—" I stop myself before saying how Mom turned catatonic. I clear my throat. "She wasn't very sentimental."

"We have another picture from Archer Omni." Porter slowly marches around the room. "It's around here somewhere."

"Do you know where Archer Omni was located?"

"Nah, we got this station from a dumpster. The lab location is hidden. You know how it is when you're working on top secret stuff." Porter pulls another pic down and hands it to me. "Ah, here it is."

I cradle the shiny paper in my palms. This one shows another angle of the Archer Omni sign. It's got a much better view of the lab as well. My mouth waters to see all the equipment. Chem stations, quantum computers, magnetic field generators... Archer Omni had all the good toys.

Next I notice someone writing on a clipboard. I pull the pic closer, trying for a better look at the person's face.

Every nerve ending in my body goes on alert.

That's no random worker. It's Miss Edith. A younger version, to be sure. But that's definitely her. As in, the kindly old lady next door—the very one who helped me watch Mom when she got out of it—was actually way more than that.

"Do you have any other pictures from that time?" I ask. I'm pretty proud how I don't get shaky voice or anything.

"Nah. All the ones we found, we taped to the wall."

"Thanks." Moving quickly, I scoop up Rakki and Bobo. "Have to run."

"Where are you going?"

"A place. To do some stuff. You know. Thanks again!"

In reality, I'm off for a talk with Miss Edith. If anyone can tell me where to find Archer Omni, she can.

As I rush across campus, I sense that shadow lurking behind me again. My muscles become sluggish and drained. Some small part of me screams to find out what that figure really is. More of me is too determined to care.

I'm about to find Archer Omni, the Andromeda Anomaly and Thorne.

Nothing else matters.

"Imprisonment is only as effective as the dungeon." - Wu Zhao Zetain, author of *The Art of Sentient War*

THE BACK WALL of my jail cell rattles. The ground shimmies beneath my feet. I summon my sentient into two forms. On my left arm, I create a shield. Meanwhile, a short sword extends from my right hand.

Whatever is coming, I'll be ready.

The wall rumbles. Distant voices scream in fear. Every inch of my jail cell vibrates with power.

All falls silent and still.

Boom!

The entire back wall explodes. I crouch behind my cover. Pings sound as stone shards slam into my shield. Distant cries sound as the locals run. I dismiss my shield and summon another short sword instead.

Not long now.

A heavy breeze sweeps away the dust that had been hazing over the scene. For the first time, I get a clear view of the street outside my prison cell. And I know who blew my jail cell open.

Justice and Slate stand just beyond the shattered wall. And they're smiling their faces off.

Slate holds up a small square box with a plunger. "Dynamite," he says.

I smile from ear to ear. "Well done."

Clearly, my brothers took the wall down with some kind of sentient-enhanced TNT. "I owe you both for this one." I dismiss both my short swords.

Justice tips his hat. "You didn't think we'd really betray you. We were working behind the scenes. You know us."

"Umbra jail," adds Slate.

There's a world of meaning in those two words.

On Earth, I heard stories about pirates who'd drop off unwanted shipmates on a deserted isle. We have a similar practice here, what's called prison planet. That's where you find a parallel universe with a deserted version of Umbra and then drop off your prisoner in manacle cords. Based on what Slate just said, my brothers must have talked Mother into locking me up here instead.

Only one thing to say to that piece of news.

"Much appreciated," I declare. "But you shouldn't have done this. You'll get in trouble."

Justice winks. "That's why you better make it worth our while."

"Plan," states Slate.

That's another single word that carries a ton of meaning. Slate wants to know if I've come up with a scheme to save Meimi and free our all our transcendents.

"I have one." Raising my hand, I open up another drift void.

"Need any help?" asks Justice.

I lift my brows in surprise. Normally, this is the part of the adventure where Justice tries to put me on a leash. Pride swells in my soul. For the first time in my life, my older brother thinks I can handle something solo.

"No," I reply. "I got this one. You two good?"

Justice chuckles. "We wouldn't have sprung you if we didn't have a plan of our own."

"Conceal," says Slate.

I nod. "Hiding out is a good idea."

"Get gone," urges Justice. There's no real heat in his voice, though. If anything, my older brother's smile has gotten bigger. "And kick some ass while you're at it."

"Transcendents," adds Slate.

No question what my younger brother means here. Slate wants Meimi, Chloe and Zoe freed.

"On it," I state.

My drift void still hangs in the air nearby. After pulling back by arm, I punch through the silver plate. A hole appears before me. It's a window to the log cabin where I left Rose Archer. I leap through. The drift void seals behind me.

It's a reflex to check what's changed since my last visit. Not much.

The rustic cabin sits on a larger swath of empty mountain range. The red desert begins just over the western hills.

I march up to the door. It opens before I can knock. A familiar face peers up at me.

"Mr. Archer." I bow slightly at the waist. This is my transcendent's father, after all. He deserves extra formality.

"Prince Thorne."

"Is Rose Archer here? I'd like to speak with you both."

"Surely." The lines of his face pull tight with worry. "But I need to make one thing clear to you first."

My blood chills. "What's wrong?"

"Once I tell you this, you may not be so keen to step inside."

Protective energy zings through my nervous system. "Have you done something to Meimi?"

"No, it's not that. When you brought Rose here, I was too concerned about her health to say anything." He inhales a long breath. "I'm not Truman Archer. I'm Professor Archibald Conway. I used to be the Head-master for ECHO Academy."

A dozen questions fly through my wind at once.

Where is Meimi's real father?

Why would an ECHO Academy guy be here?

How come I feel like my transcendent is less safe than ever?

The guy I thought was Meimi's father stares guiltily at his feet. "So you still want to come inside and talk?"

There really is only one answer to that question.

"More than ever."

23 /MEIMI

MISS EDITH, here I come!

It doesn't take me long to hack into the master hovercar system for the Boston Dome. I need even less time to program a vehicle to show that Luci and I are off for Western New Massachusetts. Sad to say, but Godwin had much better controls than Luci. It makes me wonder yet again why Conway ever trusted her to watch me.

Then again, it's working in my favor, so why worry?

Once in my hovercar, I tool along the back roads until I reach the place where I grew up. *The Ozymandias chemical plant.* It's a total ruin. I'm talking a roof that's blown off, crumbling walls and huge metal vats oozing strange-colored goo onto the sidewalk.

Ah, home.

Parking the hovercar, I head toward the small building behind the main plant. Before I left the Boston Dome, I checked the data feed to Miss Edith. It says she's still living at the same address.

I don't get halfway down the street when a low drizzle begins. *Green rain.* I forgot about that stuff. Funny the things your mind blocks when you live in the Boston Dome. Like how life off-grid smells like rotten bananas. Guess when you're here full time, the scent stops being overwhelming. What does that do to your body, anyway?

Not sure I want to know.

I pull my hoodie lower and pick up the pace. Being back here is creepy as hell. It's as if Merciless soldiers will appear with their gash guns any second. And sure, it's getting pretty dark, but I keep seeing an even deeper shadow out of the corner of my eye. It's upright and huge, like the Lacerator... Only it's not the Lacerator.

This new shadow makes my inside twist into knots. Not to mention how energy drains from my body. What's up with that?

Enough is enough. I stop in my tracks. Green drizzle soaks into my sweats. "Who's out there?"

My only reply is the continued pit-pat of rain.

"Show yourself!" I order.

At last, someone replies. "I don't know who you are, but if you don't leave my property, I'll blow your head off."

Alarm jangles down my spine. Not the response I was looking for. Why did I think it was a good idea to taunt a stalker, anyway? Little by little, I raise my hands and turn around.

Miss Edith stands behind me.

"Meimi!" She lowers her shotgun. "Come inside before you catch the new plague."

Miss Edith totters back to what was once a guardhouse for the main factory. I follow. Soon we're seated in her mini kitchen. The place hasn't changed, from the moldy walls and chipped Formica to the mismatched chairs. Miss Edith hasn't changed, either.

As I watch her brew tea, I try to align this wizened lady with the prim, organized woman I saw in the photo.

Not happening.

Miss Edith hands me a chipped cup. "Where's your young man?" She takes a seat on the opposite side of the table and blows across her own steaming mug.

"That's complicated."

"Ah, so what *would* you like to talk about?" The knowing gleam in Miss Edith's milky eyes says she already suspects what I'm about to say.

"Archer Omni. You worked there."

"I did."

"Why didn't you say anything about that?"

"It was your Mother's request. But she's not here any more."

"She's safe, you know. Just on another planet." I wince. "That must sound nuts."

Miss Edith chuckles. "As a matter of fact, it's exactly what I would have suspected. How about I tell you what *I* know?"

"Please." I grip my tea cup so hard, I'm shocked it doesn't shatter in my grasp.

"I was there in Archer Omni when it happened. It was late at night. No one else was around, just me and the Archers. There's no other way to say this." She sighs. "A space cowboy appeared."

"Actually, that makes perfect sense. Go on."

"He had some kind of black box. About this high." Miss Edith waves about three feet from the ground. He said it was a secret weapon that he needed in order to solidify his rule of the omniverse. And he asked your parents to hide it."

"That's why Thorne's family owed us a favor."

"Quite. It seems our particular flavor of reality is considered so backward, no one would think to look for this precious item here. Your parents agreed. Rose had altruistic intentions. Truman? Not so much. He broke into the box and found the swirling stuff inside. The sight scared him so much, he closed it right back up again. But the thing was never the same afterwards. Always rattling in a corner."

I wince. "That doesn't sound good."

"The big problem happened a few weeks later. That time, it was just me and Rose. The cowboy's box got out of control. Created this sheet of particles that grabbed your mother and took her to another world." Miss Edith stares into her cup. "What I'm about to say next, I've never told another soul. Not even Rose."

I lean forward. Every fiber of my body strains to hear more. "Please."

"All right," continues Miss Edith. "When Rose stepped through, the portal didn't vanish. I could watch through that connection, like I had a vid feed. Rose met some fellow on Umbra in something called a viz dome. Does that mean anything to you?"

"It does."

"The man said his name was Lucky and he kept a deck of playing cards in his fist. He said that Rose had reached the Devil's Fang and they were now buried underground. Then Lucky took Rose even deeper into the earth. They entered a crypt." Miss Edith shivers. "It was a long and low space with life pods. Lucky said the pods had run out of power to support whoever was inside them."

I gasp, remembering the image I saw when I first came back with Crown Sentient. "Were there two people?"

"Three, actually. A mother, father... and an infant."

My skin chills over in shock. "That baby was me, wasn't it?" The realization slams into me, harsh as a fist. "I'm not human."

The knowledge should make me fall from my chair. For some reason, it doesn't, Instead, the fact that I'm Umbran is comforting. Natural, even. And it explains a ton about my life.

"Lucky explained that the life support had run out on the parents, and was about to end for the child. He asked Rose to care for the girl, saying it wasn't safe for the baby to stay on Umbra."

"So Mom took me back to Earth."

Miss Edith nods. "Truman loved Botany. Said he fell for your mother because her name was Rose. We already had Luci. So Rose named you Meimi. I think it was Rose's way of trying to soften the blow that she just showed up with a newborn."

"What was my birth name?"

"Jewel."

"Jewel." I turn the word over in my mind. It feels important, yet I don't know why. *Damn.* I wish Thorne were here. He's read every book on Umbra. If anyone knew the secret of a name like Jewel, it would be my transcendent.

"I never told your mother that I saw Lucky. Afterwards, Rose hid the Archer Omni lab."

"Wait. She and Truman didn't get fired?"

"Sha. It wasn't safe for her there. Not with you. Rose was convinced someone at ECHO suspected they'd made contact with Umbra. Rose had the lab locked up and made me vow to never mention Archer Omni again. I promised myself that I wouldn't volunteer anything, but if you ever asked, I would tell the truth. And here you are."

The truth weighs on me like so many stones. "Luci said Truman resented me."

"She's not wrong. Truman thought adopting an orphaned alien was selfish. He and Rose fought something fierce."

"And it cost them their marriage. It's all my fault."

"No, your father was jealous."

My mouth falls open in shock. "Of what?"

"Rose visited another planet and adopted an alien. Trust me, if Truman had found you, it would have been a different story."

"I don't understand."

"Your mother started off as Truman's assistant. She soon became the more respected scientist. Did you know the lab began as Rose Research?"

"No, I didn't."

"Your mother changed the name to Archer Omni so Truman could feel more involved. But whether or not she adopted you, there was no way Rose would stop excelling in her own way. If it hadn't been you, something else would have set Truman off."

I lean back in my chair, sip my tea, and think things though. "Cole's tech changed Mother, didn't it?"

"Yes. Rose said that she needed to be around more sentient. It was the only way her mind could be clear."

"Why not go to Umbra? Cole owed her a favor."

"Truman had run off. Rose wouldn't leave Earth. She wanted you and Luci to have a normal life."

My skin prickles over. "So Mother stayed here, slowly losing her consciousness, all to protect me?"

"And Luci, too."

"Do you know what happened to Father?"

"No." Miss Edith takes another long sip of tea. "Rose said something once about him changing because he'd monkeyed with the black box, but she didn't say how. Maybe that was part of his problems."

For a long time, I can only stare into my cup and try not to cry. This news is glorious and horrible, all at once. The good part are all the sacrifices my mother made for me and Luci. The bad bits are, well, everything else.

Miss Edith pats my hand. "Now that's enough sad talk. Tell me about your nice man. The keeper."

I force my shoulders to straighten. "Thorne has been locked away from me. to reach him, I need to blow a hole through an exile void. Trouble is, there are no labs left with the kind of equipment I need."

Miss Edith smiles. "Now that's where I can help." Reaching around her neck, Miss Edith pulls out a chain. A small red key dangles from the end. "This opens Archer Omni. It's all been preserved for you. Rose and I wanted you to have it when you were ready."

My mind blanks from shock. "Me? Why not Luci?"

"Luci's a loser, Meimi."

I should laugh, but I can't. "Come again?"

"Your so-called sister is one lazy and mean piece of work. And Luci's dangerous, mostly because she knew she was second best to you. And so did your Mother. Honestly, how could you ever think the lab would go to Luci?"

"Mom always acted like Luci hung the sun and moon."

"Your mother tried to pump up Luci's ego. That was Rose's way of balancing the scales between you. It wasn't the best choice, but your mother did what she thought was right. I cheered when Luci ran off with Josiah."

I nod. My mind swirls through all this news. Still, I force myself to stay focused.

Thorne.

The exile void.

That's what matters.

"Where is the lab hidden?" I ask.

"Under RCM1, your old workplace." She gulps down her last bit of tea, "I hope that's all right, it being a garbage reclamation center and all."

I can't help but smile. "That's perfect."

"Before visiting another world, bring along a list of facts and questions." -
Beauregard the Great, author of *Instructions for Visiting Parallel Worlds*

AFTER STEPPING INSIDE THE CABIN, I follow Archibald over the
threshold and into a small back room lined with machines.

"I'll leave you to it," says Archibald. He leaves, closing the door
behind him. I'm left behind in a chamber that can only be described with
one word.

Wow.

I count six modified monoliths, which are multi-purpose drift science
stations. The walls are lined with stacks of slim white discs that hover
one atop the other, reminding me of so many columns on an ancient
temple. Each round item represents a separate quantum computer. A
shoulder-height silver tower—which is the latest in 3-D render boxes—
hums away in a corner. ZoomWires connect it all in a glowing web.

For a small room, this packs quite a lot of power.

Rose sits before a tall monitor, rapidly typing into a curved keyboard
that hovers before her. She doesn't look up as I approach. "Hello,
Thorne. If you don't mind, I'm in the middle of something. It won't be a
minute."

I scan her carefully. Rose is a lithe figure with gray hair and a white
lab coat. The last time I saw her, Meimi's mother was semi-catatonic.
Now, she appears like the sharp scientist Meimi always spoke about in
loving tones.

What changed?

For a few minutes, Rose pounds away at her keyboard, then slams her thumb on the return key. Her monitor flashes with a speed-scroll of calculations.

Turning, Rose focuses on me. "We have a few minutes while that runs. Why are you here?"

"I must help Meimi by finding a tower called the Devil's Fang."

Rose leans back in her chair. "That's what I figured."

"You knew this was coming? How?"

"We'll get to that in a minute," says Rose. "Any other questions?"

Not what I wanted to hear. I grip the armrests of my chair so tightly, the wood creaks under my grasp. When I next speak, it's an effort to stay calm. "Two. One, why isn't this guy the real Truman Archer? Two, where did you get Meimi? She's Umbran."

Rose's eyes narrow with a look that can only be described as *suspicious*. "I don't speak of these things, even to Meimi. And no offense, your family doesn't have the best reputation."

I gesture toward a nearby picture of Archibald. "Neither does yours."

Rose sighs. "True."

Leaning forward, I rest my elbows on my knees. "We must trust each other." I lower my voice. "This is about Meimi."

Rose nods slowly. "I'll tell you what you need to know. It all started when Truman and I did a favor for your father. We hid a device for him in Earth. It malfunctioned—"

"Unlikely."

"Correct. In all truth, my husband toyed with it and it broke."

"I must say, the more I learn about Truman, the less I like your husband."

"Agreed." Rose straightens the collar of her lab coat. "Back to my story. Due to my husband's interference, a drift void appeared which pulled me into Umbra. I landed in a vast space with a sort of three-dimensional web inside."

"We call it a Viz Dome. There aren't many of those. Were there any identifying marks?"

"An odd fellow met me there. He held playing cards."

"That would be Lucky. He claims to be King of the Sentient. I've run across him myself."

"Well, Lucky took me to this crypt under the tower. The space held three life pods. Is that regular practice?"

"Some factions keep pods in order to protect important leaders. The idea is that if they are ill, they can be revived later when we have the tech to save them. I didn't realize they were any under Devil's Fang. Then again, very little is known about that tower."

"Well, when I reached the crypt, two of the pods were out of power. The glass covers had broken open. A man and a woman were strewn on the ground, dead. Only one life pod was still functioning." Her eyes glisten with a wistful look. "It was their baby."

All the breath leaves my body. "That was Meimi?"

"Yes. Her birth name was written on the exterior." Rose exhales a shaky breath. "Jewel."

Jolts of awareness stream through my nervous system. "Say that again?"

"Jewel." Rose's eyes widen with alarm. "Why? What does that mean?"

"My home planet, Umbra, has different factions. Emperor Valerik came from the Vingian faction; Empress Alva came from the Komandir. Together, they founded the forth age of Umbra. My faction, the Oxbloods, started the fifth age. There's an old prophecy that Emperor Valerik and Empress Alva were so powerful in terms of foresight, they saw that their skills would be needed again one day. So they asked to be frozen alive along with a precious gem. When they were needed again, they would rise and wield their stone to save Umbra."

"Like the story of King Arthur and Avalon."

"Only it seems the gemstone wasn't a thing at all. It's a person... Jewel... Meimi."

"Lucky said I had to take Jewel with me or she'd die. He said I must never trust anyone with the details of her life."

Leaning back in the chair, I sort through this news. "Do you realize what this means? Meimi isn't just any Umbran. She's the unqualified royalty of both the Vingian and Komandir factions." The implications of this revelation rolls through me. "Cole."

"What do you mean?"

"My father thinks Meimi is his transcendent, not mine. Cole must know who Meimi really is."

A series of low beeps sounds. "Excuse me." Rose rises to 3D render box. "It's complete." She opens a panel atop the silver structure and pulls out a small disc. "This is a sentient compass. The location of Devil's Fang is already loaded." She crosses the space and sets the item on my palm. "Put some of your blue sentient inside; the compass will do the rest."

"Thank you." The item resembles a traditional compass, only one made of blue metal. "How did you know I'd need to visit the Devil's Fang?"

"I found Meimi there."

"Still, it's not a lock that I'd wish to return."

Rose taps her head. Blue sentient swirls in her irises. "Your father's invention changed me. When I lived on Earth, the side effect made me more catatonic by the day. Here on Umbra, I can see bits of the future sometimes."

The monitor flashes with bursts of white light. "And here we go." She returns to her chair and types away on her keyboard. "I've been working on this nonstop." The screen eases to flash. "Take a look."

Rising, I stand to gaze over her shoulder. "What's that?"

Rose gestures toward screen. "Specifics on the Andromeda Anomaly. It's a massive magnetic storm that hits in about twenty-four hours."

"Like the one you used to contact me."

"Correct. I know about this awful exile void that separates you and Meimi. And this storm?" She taps the monitor. "It's both huge and taking place right over a wormhole between our worlds. You know what Meimi will do."

I nod. "She'll use this magnetic storm to break through the exile void." I lean in and scan the numbers onscreen. "This storm won't be powerful enough on its own."

"That's why you need to be ready at precisely the time the storm is at its peak. If you both reach out across the universe at the right time—and with the magnetic storm to help—then your hands will clasp, if you get my meaning." She points to the compass in my palm. "And whatever is in Devil's Fang, it will help you both."

I want to say a million things to show my appreciation, but I can only manage two words. "Thank you."

"It's the least I can do. Your father inadvertently gave me these skills, after all." Sighing, she slumps in her chair.

I frown. "You don't look well."

"Even with my new abilities, I still have limits." Rose cups her hand by her mouth. "Archie?"

The door opens. "Are you all set?" He scans Rose's face and pales. "I can see we're all done here." He rushes to Rose's side.

"Do you need help?" I ask.

"All I can get," says Archibald. "I'm not the young man I used to be."

I scoop Rose into my arms. After Archibald leads me to her room, I set Rose atop the mattress. With gentle movements, Archibald covers her in a thin blanket. She curls onto her side.

"Will she be all right?" I ask.

"Rose will sleep for a few days, but then she'll be fine." Archibald leads me out to the main room. "You're probably still wondering why I'm here."

"I am."

"Truman Archer wanted to be headmaster. I wished to make Rose happy. Plus, Cole's tech affected Truman as well. It aged him prematurely. We ended up looking more alike than not, so it was easy to trade spots." A spot of pink appears on his long jowls. "What happens next is a little tricky."

"Allow me to guess. It involves my mother."

"That's right. Empress Janais sought out Truman Archer. She wanted her *own person* on the inside ECHO Academy. We worked out a swap." Archibald pulls at his necktie. "You should know something."

"My mother isn't very trustworthy."

"Yes, I'm so sorry."

"Never apologize for the truth." I raise the compass in my fist. "And thanks for this as well."

Archibald steps to the front door and swings it open. "Best of luck to you."

"And to you."

With that, I march off into the desert.

"ARE WE THERE YET?"

"Are we there yet?"

"Are we there yet?"

That's Zoe and Chloe, taking turns speaking from the driver's seat of my hovercar. And by *speaking*, I mean that my friends are now projected onto the camera-style lens that makes up Bobo's face. After meeting with Miss Edith, I set up a link to Chloe and Zoe. Now they're now joining me via what I've decided to call, *Bobo Cam*.

No way am I visiting Archer Omni without my besties.

Green drizzle patters on the windshield as I tool along the winding roads. Dead trees loom on either side of the cracked asphalt. Swaths of semi-solid goop hang from bare branches. For his part, Rakki skitters around the back seat, looking through the windows with interest.

At last, a familiar line of buildings appears on the horizon. *RCM-1*. It's a series of long structures made from corrugated metal. My mind blanks. For a moment, I'm nine years old once more, bumping along in a run-down bus to make my shift with Luci.

Shaking my head, I snap out of the memory. Passing by the main gate, I speed to the spot Miss Edith described: a small metal shack whose rusted door is held shut by a tiny padlock. I park the hovercar nearby.

When I look more closely into Bobo's lens 'face,' I can see more than Chloe and Zoe. Beyond them, there's the framed pictures of George Washington—a clear sign the twins are sitting in my room back in the VIP Retreat.

"Are we there yet?" asks Chloe.

"Yup." For some reason, I can only hold the steering wheel and stare at the tiny shack. Somewhere under this very stretch of ground sits Archer Omni.

My parents' laboratory.

It's still here.

And I'm about to see it.

The world takes on a dreamlike sheen. This can't be happening, and yet it is.

It's Zoe who speaks next. "You don't have to do this right now, you know."

"Yes, I do. The Andromeda Anomaly is in twenty four hours."

"Get off your ass," says Chloe.

"Language!" scolds Zoe.

Chloe huffs. "What, I can't say *ass* now?"

The sing-song nature of this familiar fight snaps me out of my funk. Straightening my back, I press the exit button on the dashboard. The front doors on the silver hovercar open upwards. Rakki, Bobo and I slip out. Light rain patters my skin. I hardly feel the touch of icky water.

My boots slog across the muddy ground as I march over to the shack. Reaching behind my neck, I pull out the same chain that Miss Edith had handed over minutes ago. I slip the key into the rusted lock, turn, and pull it out again. A low grinding sounds as the shack rolls aside, revealing a set of cement stairs that disappear into the ground.

I stare down into the darkness. The shadows seem to stare back at me. While before I felt overwhelmed, now spike of excitement moves through my soul.

I can do this.

Taking in a deep breath, I step down into the earth. A small search-light pops up from Rakki's body, illuminating my way. Once I'm deep enough into staircase, the tiny shack rolls back into place above me with a snick.

And the lights turn on.

Archer Omni is revealed.

It's a massive space lined with every kind of tech imaginable. At least a hundred tall black monoliths stand in rows like sentinels. A circle of chairs and keyboards sit around a circular column of a monitor. That's the drift hub, and it's the lab's nerve center. Dozens of small spider bots crawl all over, cleaning and repairing as they go.

My breath catches. *What a sight.*

Chloe squeals. "Do you see all this? There are quantum sensors and dark matter illuminators!" Bobo lurches over to the back right section of the room, which is chocked full of all the goodies an engineer could want.

"Bobo, over there next." Zoe points to the opposite corner. I follow her gaze, finding long white tables crammed with all sorts of small machines, vials and tools. Storage units are packed with agents and reagents of every kind.

I step around the space slowly. Rakki follows behind me, snapping pictures and making calculations as we go. Chloe, Zoe and I already mapped out our plans back at the VIP Retreat. Everything got loaded into Rakki, who's now comparing the reality of this space to the specifications we listed out. Only, I don't need to wait for Rakki's report. It's already obvious.

All the equipment we need is here. We only lack the personnel. For a project of this size, there is no way that only three people can get the job done.

Bobo toddles up to me. "This is perfect!" says Chloe from his lens face.

"Sure," I state. "Only we need help from crews at ECHO Academy. The Hobby Shop, those are your engineers, right?"

"Sort of." Chloe makes a face as she says those two words.

"And Zoe... the Cooks are your people."

Zoe winces. "I guess so."

"I can talk to Porter about getting the Guards involved." A long pause follows. "I'm not hearing the excitement, guys."

"Well, all those crews hate each other," says Chloe.

"The plan isn't super complex," I state. "But the operators need to know your stuff. These kids are the best on campus. I don't have time to babysit newbies. This is happening tomorrow night."

"Those crews won't want to even look at each other, let alone team up." Zoe sighs. "Sorry, it's just the truth."

I rub my neck and think things through. There must be something I can do here.

An idea appears.

"I've got it." I snap my fingers. "We'll invite them to the lab."

"This lab?" asks Chloe.

"Of course, it's like a super-secret national monument. They'll want to see it."

"It won't stay secret for long," adds Zoe.

"I only need them to keep their mouths shut for a matter of hours. And they will. These are the best kid scientists in the world. Once they see what we're about to do, they'll want to play with all the cool toys... and without adult supervision. I don't think anyone will blab until after the job's done."

Zoe twists the ends of her long blonde hair. "Meimi, this is impossible."

"You've said that before," I point out.

"It's never been more true than now." Chloe fixes me with a look that can only be described as miserable. "Sometimes, you just have to face realities."

When I first looked down the staircase to the lab, I'd felt a flare of excitement. Now that feeling explodes into a blaze of ferocious intent. "This Andromeda Anomaly is unique. It's the best one we'll see in *a thousand years*. What would you give decades from now for a chance to see Justice and Slate again? Can you really be happy knowing they're trapped on Umbra with Cole?

Inside Bobo's lens face, Chloe and Zoe share a long look. All the while, my heart beats at double speed. If I can't convince Zoe and Chloe to help, then I'm really sunk.

"No one thought we could save millions of lives at the Liberation Celebration," I continue. "Not even the three of us. Now we have twenty-fours, tons of equipment, and no team. But this is us. We did it before. We can do it again. I won't accept anything else. Neither should you."

Little by little, my friends turn their attention to me. Eons seem to pass before they speak again.

"We're in," they say in unison.

"Cool." I grin. "We need to invite these ECHO kids to a virtual tour of this lab. New project. Let's figure out how to get everyone here tomorrow afternoon, along with specific instructions for what they'll need to do."

Once more, we get to work.

"The forth age of Umbra shall be forever forgotten and buried." - Empress Janais, author of *The Fifth Age of Umbra*

I CHECK the small round disk in my palm once again. The circular readout shows the right coordinates. Latitude 23.806078. Longitude 11.288452.

There's no sign of the Vingian Hermitage, though.

By now, I thought I'd see some signs of the lost tower. Perhaps some artifacts in the sands. Or a spire from the top of the tower of Devil's Junction would be nice. At the very least, there should be a change in the pattern of desert—a hint at the alteration beneath.

Nothing yet.

The dual suns of Umbra beat down with a fierce heat I've never known before. Every inch of my body is covered in sweat. Frustration tightens up my neck and shoulders.

Where is this place? I check my sentient compass once more.

Latitude -24.727390. Longitude 15.342391.

Something is screwing with my sentient compass again. No doubt, there's some kind of scrambler in the sand nearby. After all, that's what I would do if I were Lucky and wanted to hide my home.

I glance once more time.

Latitude: 48.0000 Longitude: 107.0000.

Now, it's just getting annoying.

Time passes. I don't know if it's hours or days, but I do know that the heat keeps searing into me, making my legs turn wobbly. White dots blur my vision. I've been out here for too long. My water's almost gone. Some part of me screams that I should give up and go somewhere with shade.

I ignore that advice.

A low rumble cuts through the air. I've heard that noise before. Hoverbikes. Shielding my vision, I scan the landscape. A quarter mile away, a pair of hoverbikes zoom past. It must be a mirage, because I can make out the couple riding those bikes quite clearly.

It's me and Meimi.

Chances are, this is a dehydration-induced daydream. Still, it's not like I have a lot of other choices here.

I'll follow them.

The grains of sand seem to pull against my every step. Sweat streams down my back. My exposed face and hands feel as if they're on fire.

I keep marching forward.

Then I stop.

It's not on purpose.

The desert falls away beneath my feet. My breath catches. I must have hit an air pocket under the sands. These can bury you alive in minutes. On reflex, I push myself up to break free.

It doesn't happen.

Instead of passing onto firmer ground, more of the desert collapses beneath me. Hot sand quickly envelops my legs and torso. The last thing I sense is the desert encasing my head.

All becomes darkness.

THE NEXT DAY.

1:57PM

I stand beside the drift hub of Archer Omni. Ten astronaut-style chairs surround a column-shaped monitor. When you're into the hub, your work in progress shows on the pillar itself. Atop that column sits a line of small round orbs— special projectors that create holograms within the lab itself.

At 2pm on the nose, I'll turn those projectors on and see what kind of crew I'll have for tonight's Andromeda Anomaly. If I get less than thirty kids, then our chance to destroy the exile void is slim.

No pressure.

2:00 pm

I pick up my wireless keyboard and hit *enter*. A single light pulses atop the drift tower. A pair of 3-D holograms appear beside me.

Chloe and Zoe.

That's it.

My heart sinks. I'd hoped to get at least the leaders from the top crews, namely the Guards, Cooks and Hobby Shop Kids.

I shift my gaze between Chloe and Zoe. "You sent out the invites?"

"Sure," says Zoe.

"Wait," cautions Chloe. "Did you disable the security protocols?"

I lift my brows. "You're right. I forgot about that."

After slipping into one of the ten astronaut chairs, I set my keyboard into hover mode and get to work. It takes time to enter in a whole series of passwords and scans. Eventually, I'm able to hit *enter* again.

At last, a new set of orbs flare to life along the column's top. Fresh 3-

D holograms appear. This time, it's Porter Saint-Clare and two people I don't recognize. Each holds a data pad; that's how they are projecting themselves into this space.

"I'm Hoss," says the first guy. He's a towering dude who looks like he could have gone into either professional wrestling or science. "I run the Hobby Shop Kids." Hoss hitches his thumb at the girl next to him. "This is Jill Jacobs."

A petite girl with blue hair and a yellow leather onesie glares at Hoss. "I'm Chem Girl."

Hoss rolls his eyes. "Whatever you say, Jill."

I raise my hand. "You certainly look like a Chem Girl."

She nods and grins. "Thanks. I lead the Cooks."

"I was so psyched to see your invite," says Porter. "Can't wait to see what you've got cooking."

"*Cooking?*" Chem Girl sniffs. "Since when do Guards know about that?" This seems like an old fight between them.

Porter shoots her a sideways glance. "Drift science includes the mastery of chemistry, or have you forgotten?"

"So if you Guards know chemistry, does that mean you're experts in engineering, too?" asks Hoss.

"Guys!" I raise my hands, palms forward. "Let's stay focused here."

Everyone shuts their yaps. *Yay.*

"Porter is right," I continue. "I'm working on a new project, along with my friends Chloe and Zoe."

"It's going to kick major ass," says Chloe.

Zoe shoots her sister an angry look.

"What?" asks Chloe. "I thought we agreed that *ass* wasn't a swear."

It's an effort not to groan. Babysitting the crews is bad enough; I can't have Chloe and Zoe start in. Over the years, I've found it's best to cut off my friends quickly whenever they start these *what's a swear word* conversations.

I gesture around me. "This is my parents' old lab. Archer Omni."

"Whoa," says Porter. "This place was supposed to be destroyed."

"It wasn't. And we have the best toys in the history of ever." Pulling up my keyboard, I hit a button. Glamour shots of different parts of the lab appear on the monitor screen. There are the monoliths, chem stations, quantum computer servers and, of course, a pic of the astronaut chairs and drift hub. Creating this little slide show was Zoe's idea.

Based on the wide-eyed looks from Porter, Hoss and Chem Girl? *Great idea there, Zoe.*

"Here's the situation," I state. "There's another world with intelligent life and it's called Umbra. Sadly, it also has an evil Emperor named Cole who is a sadistic freak. Our mission is to topple Cole and keep Umbra safe."

"Full disclosure," adds Zoe. "Our boyfriends are Umbran princes, so we need to rescue them."

Porter frowns. "How can we help?"

"Access to Umbra is blocked right now," I explain. "To fix the Cole situation, we need to break through something called an exile void. And that will require at least ten kids from each of your crews."

"Wait, did you say *break through* an exile void?" Hoss gasps. "Does that mean humans could reach Umbra before?"

"We've been able to do that for a while," I reply. "My parents were the first to make contact, right here in this lab. But now there's this exile void problem."

"That sucks," says Chem Girl.

"There's a good side though," declares Chloe. "A magnetic storm takes place tonight at midnight. If we can tap into its energy, then Meimi can reach Umbra again. She's got some special skills that will help get the right people into power. Or to be accurate, get the bat-shit crazy guy out of power."

"Language," says Chloe.

"Meimi's got skills," Hoss repeats. His voice is a deadpan. This guy will be tough.

There's no way to sugarcoat this, so I just go for it.

"It's like this," I begin. "I can wield stuff called Crown Sentient, which are self-aware nanoparticles I stole from the emperor. If I can get to Umbra, I can hoover up the rest of his Crown Sentient and kick that sadistic kook off the throne. From there, things should be pretty easy. After all, I gave my boyfriend some Crown Sentient back in Umbra. Logic says I can toss it at whoever I choose. Someone will want to be emperor or empress. Long story short, we'll worry about the *who rules the omniverse* question later. The emperor is the big problem now."

A long pause follows. *Oops*. Maybe I over-shared. There's nothing I can do to take it back now, so I press another button on my keyboard.

"You'll see a manual come up on your data pads," I continue. "As I said before, we need ten of the best kids from each of your crews. These instructions will tell them what to do."

On the holograms, I see Porter, Hoss and Chem Girl lift their data pads and flip through the screens. I give them a minute before going on.

"What do you say?" I ask.

Silence.

"I know this seems a little out there," I add. "But I swear, my parents really did this. Umbra is totally a *thing*. If you want, I can do a demonstration."

This is the part I've been dreading, by the way. Sure, I can use my Crown Sentient for some magic tricks. Trouble is, using Crown Sentient on Earth gives me a migraine of epic proportions. I need to save up the pain for when it's really needed.

And that's tonight at twelve, when the magnetic storm is at its peak.

"You don't need to do anything," says Porter. "Just seeing inside this lab is enough."

"Yeah," agrees Hoss.

"I believe you, too," adds Chem Girl.

"So is that a *yes* on helping?" I ask. "Remember, you'll be interacting with another world. That's beyond cool."

"Not if the Cooks are in on it." Porter folds his arms over his chest. "Chem Girl put some silver goop in our swimming pool. The Guards turned purple for a week."

Chem Girl Smirks. "Eh, you loved it."

"You're one to talk." Hoss wags his finger at to Porter. "The Guards poured sand in our atomic slicer. Took a month to clean."

Even in the hologram, it's clear how Porter's face turns pink. "We only did that because the Hobby Shop Boys nailed our furniture to the ceiling."

Hoss shrugs. "You got it down again."

From there, the chorus of complaints grows louder. Everyone talks on top of each other. Too bad these guys are really the best of the best. Chloe, Zoe and I checked through all the other profiles at school. Anyone else would need weeks to train before jumping in and helping out.

"Whoa," I declare. "We don't have time for this. The Andromeda Anomaly reaches its peak at midnight tonight."

Yet the whining continues.

Chloe sets her pinkies at either side of her mouth and lets out an ear-piercing whistle. Everyone falls silent.

Chloe gestures to me. "They're all yours, Science Bitch."

"Language," whispers Zoe.

"Look," I continue. "You all have grudges against each other. I get that. But underneath it all, I know that you're truly scientists at heart."

"I am," says Chem Girl.

"She's not," report Hoss and Porter in unison.

"That's enough," I declare. "If you're interested in taking part in this super-awesome space project, then come to this lab at midnight. The coordinates are on your data pads. And please say nothing about this to anyone."

Chem Girl sets her fist on her hip. "I won't be here if—"

"Oh no!" I cry. "Bad connection." I click another button on my keypad and shut off the link to Hoss, Porter and Chem Girl. For a long moment, Zoe, Chloe and I merely stare at each other in silence.

Damn. That did not go well.

"The experience of the present is merely an illusion for human minds. When it comes to sentient, the past, present and future all exist at once." - Hammurabi the Seventh, author of *Law of Sentient*

HOT SAND PRESSES into my limbs, mouth and eyes, keeping me trapped in place. With every passing moment, my lungs ache for fresh oxygen. Little by little, particles fall out below my feet. I slowly seep downward.

Then I break free.

Darkness surrounds me as I tumble through empty space. Blessed air flows into my lungs. I summon my battle sentient to thicken my body armor. With a thud, I land against cold stone. After I cough out sand, I wait for my vision to adjust to the shadows around me.

At last, things come into focus.

I've landed in a long stone chamber. Tattered banners hang from the ceiling, each one decorated with a swirl of scrolls—the signet for the forth age of Umbra. Against the far wall, a trio of glass life-pods rest upon a high altar. A single pool of light surrounds the spot.

I move closer.

Two adult-sized pods flank either side of the stone altar. The once-broken glass has been reformed into a cracked sheath, so it's no longer possible to see inside. Still, one thing is clear—a single person rests within each pod.

I sigh. Between my first visit with Lucky and my last talk with Rose Archer, the identity of these two bodies is clear.

These are Meimi's parents.

A small pod sits between the two larger ones. Its glass top is gone, revealing an interior lined with read-out screens and controls. I brush my fingers along the writing set into the outside.

Jewel.

That's Meimi's Umbran name. Being here makes me feel closer to my transcendent and yet at the same time, I'm trapped universes away. My soul aches.

A voice sounds behind me, interrupting my thoughts.

"Greetings, Prince Thorne."

I've only heard this particular tone once before. Even so, it's unmistakable. Turning around, I encounter a familiar face.

"Hello, Lucky." He looks unchanged from our last meeting, what with his gangly body, slicked-back hair, and fitted suit.

"Do you believe in fate?" asks Lucky.

"No, I don't."

Lucky lowers his voice. "Well, I *am* fate."

I shrug. "Still don't believe."

A small smile curls Lucky's mouth. "How wise."

"I must break the exile void between me and Meimi. I need your help."

Lucky flips playing cards between his palms in a seesaw motion. "Ask me the right questions and I will."

Easy enough.

"I know who Jewel is," I begin. "But do you know who *I* am?"

Lucky's cards contract into a deck that sits in his right hand. Seems like that question got quite a reaction.

"You, Thorne Oxblood, are Princess Jewel's true transcendent."

I step closer. "And why would the Sentient King care about that?"

"That's another good question, so I will answer. The thing is, I've seen the future."

"That seems to happen a lot with sentient."

"Your brother Slate and I shall fight one day. Let's just say I owe your family a favor." He arches his dark brows. "One last question."

I set that little nugget of news aside to share with Slate at another time. Right now, there is indeed one last big question to ask.

"Where is the Vingian viz dome?"

Lucky winks. "Follow me."

Turning, the Sentient King marches off through a nearby archway and into a maze of nearby tunnels and stairs. It's hours of huffing and climbing. Finally, we step through another long tunnel and into a vast and darkened space. A familiar rush of power surrounds me. No question where we are.

The Vingian viz dome.

Lucky pauses. "You're on your own from now on. Maybe." Black sentient surround him in a cloud. One moment, Lucky is a swirl of small particles. The next, he's gone.

Which is fine with me.

I've got stuff to do. Closing my eyes, I summon my Crown Sentient with an inner vow.

Meimi, I will see you again.

11:51 pm

It's only me, Chloe and Zoe in Archer Omni... and nine minutes before we need to tap into the Andromeda Anomaly. Anxiety twists through me.

This doesn't bode well.

Nervous energy has me all fidgety. It's an effort to keep my butt in my fave astronaut chair while I type away on my keyboard. Meanwhile, Zoe and Chloe race around the lab. Rakki chases Chloe while Bobo does the same with Zoe.

Atop the podium, I programmed a little progress bar showing how much more needs to get done before we can tap into the Andromeda Anomaly.

We've only got 13% of our tasks done. *Yuck.*

At last, the lab door swings open. I exhale. *Finally.* Some of the crew have arrived.

Rising, I turn to scan the entrance. Two people have indeed arrived, only they aren't from any crew.

It's Luci and Conway.

Sweet mother of science.

"A viz dome is the ultimate tool to guard and garden the omniverse." - Wu Zhao Zetain, author of *The Art of Sentient War*

I STEP AROUND in a slow circle. The Vingian viz dome stretches around me. What a deep and impossibly large space. A constant hum of power presses into my skin, reminding me how this is the most powerful viz dome in the omniverse.

Presences seem to lurk in the depths around me, hidden eyes that leer out from the darkness. Sure, it could be my mind playing tricks on me.

Somehow, I doubt it.

Lucky may have promised to leave, but he could always hide nearby if he wished. After all, that's what I did when I visited this same spot during my trip through time.

Ah, well. If Lucky hides nearby, there's not much I can do about it. And the Andromeda Anomaly starts in a matter of minutes.

This may be my only chance to see Meimi again.

I'm taking it.

11:51 pm

My stomach sinks. Conway and Luci are really here.

In my secret lab.

And the ECHO crews aren't.

What a disaster.

It takes everything in me not to scream. I glance to the top of the drift hub monitor.

16%

11:52 pm

Crown Sentient churn through me, calling out to be used as a weapon against my latest obstacle. At the same time, pain bites into my temples. Particles swirl above my skin. I force the sentient back into my flesh.

Not yet.

For his part, Conway saunters into the lab, surveying it with an expert eye. He's sporting his classic tweed suit and an angry look on his mushy face. "I didn't know this place still existed. Imagine my surprise when I intercepted some illegal communications that claimed a destroyed lab was still in working condition."

Luci straightens the lapels of her overly large trench coat. "*Meimi* knew the lab was here all along."

I roll my eyes. "Because I was a sneaky genius baby."

Chloe and Zoe stare at me from their corners of the lab. The questions are there if unasked. *Do we go on?*

I make shoo fingers at them and smile. It's my way of saying, *keep at it —I've got this.* My friends get back to work.

Conway stalks closer. "You're certainly a devious teenager, considering how you slipped away from Luci."

"Right." Ignoring Conway and Luci, I return my attention to my keyboard. There's not a lot of time and tons to do. If I don't make contact with Thorne, it won't be because Luci and Conway distracted me.

"You're very naughty," states Conway. "Don't you think?"

I pound away at my work. "Are you still talking?"

"Explain yourself," snaps Conway. "I told you to accept Luci's oversight."

"Not my fault," I counter. "You shouldn't have trusted her. Luci's not a professional guard."

From the corner of my vision, I watch a wide and genuine smile stretch its way across Conway's face. Even his jowls crease from the movement.

"Of course, I trust her," declares Conway. "She's my *blood* daughter."

My fingers stall over the keyboard. *I must not have heard that right.* Across the room, Chloe and Zoe move at double speed. I can almost picture the thought bubbles over their heads saying, *noo nee noo nee noo, nothing to see here.*

They really are the best buddies ever.

I round on Conway. "She's your *what?*"

It's Luci who answers the question, and she shares the same overly-happy grin as Conway.

"He's *my* father." To emphasize this point, Luci winds her arm through Conway's. "Truman Archer helped emperor Cole hide some secret weapon. Doing so made father's age early, which is devastating to anyone. Afterwards, *my* father just sat around, catatonic."

I pull on my ear, as if this movement will somehow jump start my brain into understanding all this. Doesn't work.

"But *your* father wasn't catatonic," I clarify.

"Not technically," counters Luci. "But he was really upset."

"Our Mom was actually catatonic," I continue. "You remember that, don't you?"

"Of course! Mom got zapped by the same tech."

"So Mom was *really* hurt by Cole's secret gizmo while this guy—" here I gesture in the general direction of Conway "—just sat around feeling sorry for himself because he looked older."

Conway sniffles. "I was shattered."

Thankfully, my friends now decide to step in.

"Don't most scientists want to look older and stuff?" asks Chloe.

"Right on, sister," adds Zoe. "Gray hair is hot." Zoe glances toward Conway while making her *eew-face*. "Not on you obviously, because your personality is just, you know..."

"Shitty," finishes Chloe.

Zoe nods. "Yes, that."

It's a big deal for Zoe to allow an actual swear word to slip by. I appreciate the sign of support.

Luci walks over to a nearby stretch of wall. Reaching up, she pulls down a web of ZoomWires. Sparks fly. High-pitched snaps slice through the air. A monolith supercomputer goes dark.

I gasp. "What are you doing?"

"Exercising my rights," states Luci. "This is my lab is mine as much as yours."

"Hold on, there." Rising, I hold my arms up and palms forward. It's a gesture I've seen in hostage negotiation vids. "This guy over there is my father. I'm still processing that."

Zoe nods. "Me, too."

"Me, three," adds Chloe.

Conway narrows his eyes. "I am *not* your father. You're *my* predator."

Chloe and Zoe look to me. The words are there if unspoken, *what will we do here?*

No question on that score. I'll must incapacitate Conway and Luci. Besides, we're stuck at 17% with only seven minutes left to go. Tapping into the Andromeda Anomaly might not work, but I'm still not missing my chance because of Luci and Conway.

I wave to my bots. "Rakki, Bobo, get your zappers out." Both little mechanical friends lift their tiny arms.

"Back off," says Luci. She pulls two long items out from under her coat. My breath catches.

Luci has gash guns.

What the ever loving hell?

Moving swiftly, Luci points her first weapon right at my face.

Oh, no.

These are the same weapons the Merciless leverage. Gash guns tear huge holes in anything they target. Luci aims her second weapon at the wall of equipment behind Chloe.

Click, click. BAM!

An entire panel of equipment explodes. Dark matter detectors, magnetic sensors, ZoomWires... it all goes up in smoke.

"Come on!" I throw my hands up. "We have six minutes to open the drift void and connect to Umbra. The Andromeda Anomaly has a single peak. One. This is our only chance for a thousand years."

"Boo hoo." Luci points the gash gun at Zoe's chem station.

Click, click. BAM!

Luci blows up six feet of precious lab table. Green smoke rises into the air. Yellow acid spills across the floor.

"Come on," I cry. "We don't have enough people as it is. We're almost out of time. You can do whatever you want to me, just let Zoe and Chloe finish connecting with Umbra."

Or rather, attempting to do so. Not that I'm explaining that to Luci and Conway.

Zoe and Chloe nod, their eyes wide and expectant.

For her part, Luci looks to Conway. "What do you say, father?"

Conway grins, showing off a mouth of crooked yellow teeth. *Eek.* I thought ECHO Academy would have a dental plan. "Take down the drift hub."

Bands of terror tighten around my chest. "NO! We can't do anything without that!"

Luci aims the gash gun at the hub. The movement only takes a moment, but every shift and rise seems to take forever to happen.

Click, click...

But before the gash gun can discharge, something unexpected happens.

Both Luci and Conway fall over.

My eyes widen as I see what's caused the change. Chem darts protrude from Luci and Conway's necks. And when I say chem, I mean those of the tranquilizer variety. I should know. I've had these tossed my way before.

Turning, I see who chucked the tranqs in the first place and grin.

The ECHO crews are here.

They actually showed.

I quickly count heads. Exactly thirty students stand at the entrance, ten from each crew. Each holds a print out of our manuals in their fists. Worry unwinds inside me. This is exactly what we need. Porter, Hoss and Chem Girl stand in front of each group.

Never been happier to see anyone.

Chem Girl waves in my direction, a motion which shows off the chem dart still held in her fist. "Hey, Meimi."

I bow my head slightly, because that tranq trick was simply too cool. "Chem Girl."

"Uh, Jill—" begins Porter.

"It's Chem Girl," she corrects.

Porter takes off his straw fedora and fans himself. "Chem Girl, you just took down our headmaster."

She shrugs. "So what? We're opening up outer space."

"That's right," I state. "I'm guessing you all know your stations?"

"Yup," says Chem Girl.

"I guess," adds Hoss.

"Totally ready," declares Porter.

I rub my palms together. "In that case, let's fire it up."

We have five more minutes.

"There is no agony to match that of a transcendent that's been separated from the other half of their soul." - Empress Ophelia, author of *The Lost Book of Transcendence*

THE MOMENT TAKES on a dreamlike sheen. I've really done it; I found the Vingian viz dome. And the Andromeda Anomaly is almost at its peak.

So close.

"Begin," I command.

The viz dome responds. Threads of white timelines whip around me, creating a three-dimensional web. Brightness shifts along each line—it's the sentient's way of showing the past, present and future of different parallel universes.

Excitement zings though my nervous system.

One of these threads is Meimi's world, I know it.

Crown sentient churn though my soul. I call upon that power within me. Particles rise up from my flesh and swirl above my skin. Energy zings through my limbs. My body grows larger. Bones stretch and muscles bulge.

"Show me Meimi," I order.

A moment passes. Pressure and worry press in around me, tight as vise.

Suddenly, one of the threads shines with crimson light. Hope sparks in my heart.

There it is. Meimi's world.

I grasp the thread. Normally, this motion would transport me to

Meimi's side. But there's an exile void at work here. Instead of moving me to my destination, a plate of red sentient hover in the air. I punch at the void, testing to see if it will hold. My knuckles come back bloody. The drift void remains the same.

Solid.

Unmovable.

Not acceptable.

"Tap into the power of the Andromeda Anomaly," I command.

My Crown Sentient lift from my skin and flow into exile void before me. Power thrums through every nerve ending in my body. Although I'm taller and stronger, my body aches as if each cell is being torn apart. Gritting my teeth, I keep my focus on the red exile void before me.

Little by little, the crimson particles become semi-transparent. A dim outline is visible through the exile void.

Almost there.

"Look my way," I whisper. "See me, Meimi."

And I wait.

THE ARCHER OMNI is a buzz of action. Cooks brew up all sorts of foams and gels. Hobby Shop Kids race back and forth around their maze of equipment. The Guards in their ten astronaut chairs, typing furiously onto their keyboards.

I check the column in the center of the drift hub.

11:57 pm

82%

To my right, a shimmer appears in the air, reminding me of heat currents on a summer day. I blink hard, trying to clear my vision.

Am I seeing things?

11:58 pm

93%

The Andromeda Anomaly is about to begin. I need to check everyone's work, not worry about optical illusions.

That's when it happens. Feelings flow through me. They aren't my own.

There's the zing of excitement.

Ache of worry.

Pang of desire.

My legs turn wobbly beneath me. No question about it. Those feelings come from Thorne. I'm sensing him again. My eyes mist over.

The shimmer in the air moves more violently. That can't be an illusion. It's Thorne. My heart soars.

From the corner of my vision, I also notice a long shadow seeping in through the entrance to the laboratory. The weak feeling in my legs moves throughout my entire body. Part of my mind screams this is dangerous.

More of me can't wait to see my transcendent again.

I check the wall clock.

11.59 pm

98%

"Everyone!" I cry. "On my mark."

The room of students falls silent. Zoe and the Cooks wait in one corner of the room. Chloe and her Hobby Shop Kids stand in the opposite space. And the Guards sit at the drift hub.

Everyone is quiet. Holding their breath. Hands poised for their work. Waiting for my signal.

I keep my eyes glued to the clock.

"Bring forth the drift void," I cry. "Three, two, one!"

Everyone launches into action. Before me, the heat-like shimmer in the air transforms into a full drift void—a round circle of red particles. The circle glitches in and out of existence. One moment, the plate of sentient are red and solid. The next, the void is silver and hollow in the center.

All of a sudden, I can't pull in enough air. Somehow, I force out another command. "Pump in more power. It's not stable yet."

Across the lab, students launch into various tasks. Guards type in fresh code. The Hobby Shop Kids fire up new equipment, which begins to glow orange from heat and strain. The Cooks rushes over to spray equipment with white foam. The heated items soaks in coolant as soon as it hits the super-heated surfaces.

Lights blink overhead. An otherworldly wind strikes up inside the lab, whipping papers and glass vials about. Crashes sound. Machines moan under the stress.

Before me, the drift void keeps flipping between solid red... and a clear portal that opens straight through to Umbra. Bit by bit, I can even see both aspects of the void more clearly. On one side, there is the Archer Omni lab. On the other is a vast and dark chamber.

And Thorne.

Our gazes lock. More emotions move through me.

A rush of joy.

Heat of affection.

Underpinning of rock-solid strength.

"More power," I cry.

"We'll bring it," calls Chloe. She's playing it tough, but there's no mistaking the undercurrent of fear in her voice.

A memory appears. When I first opened the drift void to Thorne, Mother and I blew apart our secret lab. Zoe and Chloe would tell me if she was pushing things too far, wouldn't they?

The machines rattle. Beams of red light peek through the metal seams. Students keep working away. Spraying foam. connecting mono- liths in a greater web of power. Typing in fresh code into the drift science hub. They are calm and determined.

Now I add my energy into the mix. "Sentient, deploy!" Particles whip up from my skin and soak into the drift void before me. Pain spikes through my head. I won't stop.

Suddenly, the glitching ends. A wide hole opens before me.

"We did it!" I cry. "Stabilize the connection."

There's no question what should happen next. Chloe can reduce her power. Zoe should spray more coolant.

At last, I will enter Umbra.

That's when the shadow behind me jumps out. It's no longer a mystic form either. This is a figure that's both solid and angry. My breath catches.

Oh, no.

"Nothing compares to the joy of transcendents reuniting." - Empress Ophelia, author of *The Lost Book of Transcendence*

FOR ONE MOMENT, everything is perfect. The drift void opens to a laboratory on earth. I vaguely register that the place is packed with cool tech. Still, all my attention stays locked on Meimi.

She stands on the other side of the drift void.

Beautiful.

Beaming.

My transcendent.

Then her body changes. Dark particles fly off her skin. The movement is too fast for most people to see, but I can tell what's happening. That's because I now wield Crown Sentient, too. And because of that, there's no question in my mind.

Crown Sentient are leaving Meimi. Her stance wobbles. No doubt, the fact that Meimi is losing sentient makes her feel weak. At the same time, the particles whip across the room to form a shadow. It's like a sentient swarm, only far more dense.

The semi-transparent shape then solidifies into familiar outline.

Cole.

Every muscle in my body tightens with alarm. Cole moves with hyperspeed. To everyone else in Meimi's lab, they'll just see a blur of motion. For my part, I can make out the movements as Cole races across the room and throws Meimi over his shoulder in a fireman's hold.

Cole raises his arm and opens a new drift void. No question what this means. He's taking Meimi and running to somewhere on Umbra.

No doubt, it won't be the Vingian viz dome

My thoughts rush through this turn of events. For days, Cole has been hiding out in his forge. I'd wondered what he was up to. Now I know. Cole somehow built a system to connect with Meimi's Crown Sentient. Then Father waited until Meimi and I broke through the exile void ourselves. Now he's taking advantage of our work to take Meimi from me.

Not on my watch.

Back on Earth, Cole takes out his sentient gun and blasts through a line of monoliths in Meimi's lab. Six burst into flame from his single shot. Lab lights flicker before going dark.

Cole races through the fresh drift void she just created. At the same time, I rush into action, racing through my own drift void to land inside Meimi's lab.

Cole and Meimi are half-way through the new drift void when I leap in behind them, tackling Cole onto the ground on the other side of his own portal.

It's instantly clear where Cole has taken us.

Fort Derringer.

And not just any place here, but we've arrived right in front of Cole's forge. This is the very same secret lab where Father has been building his tech and schemes.

No time to worry about those now.

Wrapping my arms around Meimi's waist, I yank her away from Cole. All around us, my people run off in all directions. Many crying out for a good place to hide.

Smart citizens.

"Hand over my bride," snarls Cole.

"Never," I state.

Beside me, Meimi slips from my hold to stand straight and tall. "Not a fan of that idea, either."

The ground rumbles for a moment. My mind blanks. I've experienced this before, and it's not fun.

Great manacle cords erupt from the earth, wrapping up me, Cole and Meimi.

"How are you doing this?" asks Cole.

"I'm not," I state.

The forge doors swing open, revealing another person in our midst.

Janais.

"This is my doing," she announces.

Cole pales. "What did you do to my forge?"

"Interesting new decorations, husband." Janais pushes the barn-style doors wide open, revealing what's inside.

Meimi cranes her neck toward the forge. When she next speaks, her voice is a low whisper. "No."

I follow Meimi's line of vision. *Damn.* Father has set up a familiar bunch of equipment inside his lab. There's an operating table and some mindwash machines. I've seen these before.

It's the same stuff Doc Godwin used to wipe Meimi's memory.

Pure rage courses through me. I've heard about people seeing red, but that's what actually happens to me in this moment. My father's plan becomes clear. He locked Meimi off behind an exile void, which gave him time to set up his own mind wipe equipment. Then Father waited until Meimi and I broke open the exile void ourselves so Cole could drag Meimi to his lab.

If kidnapping and mind washing bother Cole, he doesn't show it. Instead, my father glares at Janais.

"Manacle cords are my invention," snarls Cole. "They can't hold me for long."

"I don't need much time." Janais steps in a slow line before us. "I don't have Crown Sentient, but I've enough power to take care of this awful situation."

"What do you plan to do?" I ask.

Janais lifts her arm and opens another drift void. "My husband and son, you two have quite a treat coming. You're about to share your very own prison planet." Janais turns to Meimi.

"And you?" asks Mother. "You're going to hell."

Beside me, Cole struggles under the manacle cords. Then he breaks loose. My father's first act to tear away the manacle cords from Meimi.

Janais rushes forward, grasps Meimi's shoulders, and pushes her to the ground. Then she goes toe-to-toe with Cole. "How dare you choose another? I'm your empress."

Cole's mouth thins to an angry line. "You're the one who watched while my true transcendent was killed."

Janais pales. "What?"

"The Crown Sentient showed me everything!" cries Cole.

While my parents keep yelling, Meimi slowly rises to stand. Her gaze locks with mine. All the determination in the omniverse shines in my transcendent's eyes. She tilts her head with an unspoken question. *Should I?*

I nod. *Yes.*

To be sure, I've no idea what Meimi plans to do. That said, my parents are now grossly underestimating Meimi's abilities. If I'm freed from these manacle cords, then my parents will pay attention. But my parents expect little from Meimi. She's in the perfect position for a stealth attack.

And although Meimi's not a trained warrior, she's both ticked off and packed with Crown Sentient.

Sure enough, my girl goes into attack. Crown Sentient particles swirl above her skin, turning into long cords. Quick as lightning, Meimi links these long lines directly into Cole and Janais' skin. For a moment, I'm not sure what Meimi is up to.

Then I realize it. She's asked the Crown Sentient to take the form of ZoomWires.

My girl is downloading herself some power.

A great burst of sentient erupts around my parents, then moves along Meimi's ZoomWires to career right into her body. My parents hunch over and writhe.

A great burst of light erupts around Meimi as she takes in all the Crown Sentient. Then another ZoomWire erupts from Meimi's palm. This one attaches right to my chest.

Instead of draining me, the ZoomWire sends Crown Sentient rushing into my body. Power swells within my soul. Using that energy, I burst through the manacle cords holding me down.

More and more Crown Sentient pour into me and Meimi. Then it stops. Meimi pulls back her sentient ZoomWires. My parents are free, but now without any Umbran power at all. Turning, they both run.

And they fall right into the drift void Mother created before. My parents tumble through to a deserted prison planet. The drift void closes.

Humans would call that karma. Umbran say it's sentient. Either way, it's a fitting end.

With hobbling steps, Meimi and I move toward each other. Our bodies press and arms wrap about each other. I decide that nothing will be sweeter—whether in this life or the next—than holding my transcendent in this moment.

"It's over," whispers Meimi. "There's no one left to fight."

I freeze. The locals have come back out of hiding. Leaders of opposing factions now stand on the nearby stretch of street—Doc Pyotr from the Komandir and Locus from the Vingians.

And one thing I can say for both of them? They definitely look ready for battle.

THORNE AND I EMBRACE.

This should be the *happy ending and hugging* part of my life.

Not exactly.

A group of Umbrans lurk nearby. Some dress as cowboys and cowgirls. Others seem like they just came offstage on a Wild West floorshow. More wear simple white robes. Yet although they all dress differently, these Umbrans have one thing in common.

They look like hungry dogs salivating over fresh steak. And in this scenario, Thorne and I are the red meat.

Thorne raises his hands. "Listen to me. My parents are gone. I'm sure you all have questions about what happens with imperial rule. Let me assure you, everything is absolutely fine."

The crowd calms down a bit. *Go Thorne.*

My transcendent continues. "As you all saw with your own eyes, Meimi and I took in Crown Sentient. There is no reason to be con—"

Suddenly, blue sentient rise up from Thorne's skin, encasing him in a haze of azure. He freezes.

Reaching out, I rest my hand on Thorne's arm. "Are you all righ—"

Now azure-colored sentient rise up from my own skin. Every inch of my body ceases to move. Blue light now surrounds both me and Thorne. The sight of the street and angry Umbrans all vanish. Around us, the brightness flares until Thorne and I are surrounded in nothing but beams of color.

My parents appear. And by this, I don't mean Rose and Truman Archer. Instead, there's a man in white robes who stands beside a woman in a bright purple dress. She wears a top hat and holds a bronze cane.

More light flares in my father's arms. And there I am. Baby Meimi.

A memory appears. I recall when the Lacerator appeared to me back in that metal container during the Liberation Celebration. I saw a pair of dead figures, and the sight caused me pain.

These were the two people I saw. My birth parents.

Cold grief seeps through my soul. I shiver. Thorne must sense my emotions, because he sets his palm against the base of my spine. His touch helps to keep me centered.

The emperor bounces Baby Me in his arms. "You are our jewel."

"Jewel?" I ask.

Thorne pulls me closer. "That's your birth name."

"Jewel," I repeat. "It's... nice."

"We were the first rulers of the Fourth Age of Umbra," says the empress. "After you were born, we placed ourselves and you into life pods. Your father and I didn't survive, but you did. That's what matters."

I frown. "Why would you freeze yourselves?"

"Because we saw the future," adds the emperor. "Over the thousands of years of the forth age, we got visions of how various emperors and empresses would stop fully sharing Crown Sentient and power. That causes imbalances." He looks to Thorne. "You've seen for yourself what can result."

Thorne nods. "The imperial family is here to guard and garden the omniverse. Some rulers began wiping out entire worlds without good reason." He shakes his head. "That's simply wrong. All life matters."

A shock of awareness skitters across my skin. "Did Cole do that as well?"

"He did," answers Thorne.

As my transcendent says these two words, he seems all things calm and regal. Yet I can sense his inner turmoil. This isn't easy for him.

The empress grins. "You've made us proud."

"Both of you," adds the emperor.

A fresh burst of blue light surrounds us. When the flare of brightness vanishes, my birth parents are gone. Instead, there stands a lanky guy in a fitted suit. He grips a deck of playing cards in one hand.

The man bows to me. "Pleasure to meet you, Jewel. I'm King of the Sentient. You can call me Lucky." He glances to Thorne. "Hello, again."

Beside me, I sense Thorne stiffen his stance. Whoever this Lucky fellow is, my transcendent doesn't trust him.

"What do you want?" asks Thorne.

"To finish my task, of course. I set all this up so you can repair the damage done during the forth age of umbra."

"Repair?' I ask. "What does that mean?"

Lucky flips his cards from one palm to the other. "Glad you asked. It means this."

Another flare of blue light erupts. At the same time, Lucky himself explodes into a cloud of colored particles.

All of those tiny bits fly straight for me and Thorne. I watch in shock as the particles swirl across our skin. These are the same moving tattoos that I saw whenever taking in Crowne Sentient.

Now we're soaking in power from the Sentient King himself.

Energy churns inside me. A headache bites into my temples, worse than anything I'd ever felt before.

And that's when things get really weird.

"How many ages of Umbra will ultimately come to pass? None can say." - Beauregard the Great, author of *Instructions for Visiting Parallel Worlds*

I CAN'T BELIEVE that just happened. Lucky transformed into more sentient and actually entered both me and Meimi.

Talk about the unexpected.

Tons of images and facts flit through my mind at what feels like light speed. None of them are coming from my own mind.

It's all Lucky.

I see worlds collide, stars fade, and futures collapse. Every fact and facet leads to a single conclusion.

Meimi and I are meant to be emperor and empress.

The blue light flares once more. Lucky's sentient self rises up from both me and Meimi. The many particles fly away, reforming into the shape of Lucky once more.

"You know what to do?" asks the Sentient King.

Meimi and I share a long look. When we speak again, it's in unison. "Yes."

"Good," says Lucky. "In that case, you're ready."

Colored brightness surrounds us again. This time, it's so intense my head hurts.

When the light fades, Meimi and I are back at Fort Derringer. A small crowd still surrounds us. It's Doc Pyotr who speaks first.

"Y'all okay?" he asks.

"Yes." Meimi and I reply together.

It must be a side effect of our new Crown Sentient, but Meimi and I know precisely what to do next. There's no need for conversation or planning. Lucky's visions showed us enough. And through our transcendent bond, I can sense that Meimi is just as certain about this as I am.

So we get to work.

Harnessing our new Crown Sentient, Meimi and I summon the mother of all drift voids. Then we change the very geography of both our home worlds. Using our sentient power, I bring up the Devil's Fang from the depths of the red desert. Meanwhile, Meimi rebuilds and repairs a place called the Tusk. We summon both structures to this very street on Fort Derringer. Meimi conjures long ZoomWire-style tendrils that bring the buildings together.

A flurry of Crown Sentient rise into the air, creating a column of particles that reach into the clouds. When the pillar lowers, there's a new construction in the center of Fort Derringer.

It's combination of the Devil's Fang and the Tusk.

A sense of satisfaction winds through me. The new tower is split down the center, with half being the black stone of the Devil's Fang, while the other half gleams with glass from the Tusk.

Minutes ago, the Umbran factions were wondering who should take the imperial crown. Now, they stare at the new building with wide eyes and open mouths.

Meimi raises her arms. "My Emperor and I have unified Earth and Umbra. This building is both our castle and the permanent connection between these two worlds."

I shoot her a sly smile. "My Emperor?"

Neither of us wanted to rule anything, let alone a combination of Umbra and Earth. But after taking in all this sentient? We now know the truth. This has always been meant to happen.

And even better, it feels right.

Meimi goes up on tiptoe and kisses my cheek. "Yes, you're all mine."

Warmth and love spread through my chest. "As you are to me."

I offer Meimi my hand. She links our fingers and together, we step into the first floor of our new palace tower. Once again, there's no need for discussion. Meimi and I already know what we'e about to do.

Hold our very first court as emperor and empress.

Thorne and I step into our new tower. As we walk forward, the filaments shape the main room. It becomes a large and empty space. One side of the room is dark stone, the other all windows.

A short flight of steps appear by the far wall. These stairs end in a pair of silver chairs. Thorne and I ascend the steps and take our seats, side by side. Lucky gave me the power to better manipulate my Crown Sentient, so I command them to transform my clothes. What were once sweats now become a long white gown with a red sash. For his part, Thorne wears a black military jacket, leather pants and tall boots.

Once we're seated, a whirl of sentient appear at the base of the stairs. It's Lucky.

"Miss me?" he asks.

"I thought we weren't seeing you again," I state.

"The pair of you are rather entertaining," says Lucky. "I've decided to spend more time in your company."

"In that case, *we may be* the ones with good fortune."

Thorne shoots me a sly grin when he says the words *we may be*. Both of us aren't certain what team the Sentient King really plays for. Does he truly care for the fate of life in the omniverse? Who knows?

Thorne and I wave our arms. The front doors from the dark stone side of the palace swing open, revealing the streets of Fort Derringer. With hesitant steps, Umbrans slip into the chamber. Lucky announces each entrant.

There's Justice, Slate, Doc Pyotr and Locus.

And finally, my mother steps into the chamber. She looks all things bright eyed and happy. The real Archibald Conway walks along at her side. My visions from Lucky explained their relationship to me and I'm totally on board. My mother deserves all the joy in the universe.

"Still seems a little empty in here," says Lucky.

"What do you suggest?" I ask.

"I'll summon some more friends. This is a rather important day, after all."

Another set of doors swing open. This time, the opening is from the glass side of the building. Beyond the threshold, I make out the familiar landscape of the ECHO Academy campus.

Again, Lucky announces everyone.

There's Chem Girl, Hoss and Porter Saint Clare.

Then follows Miss Edith, President Hope, and the Hollow.

As every visitor enters, they carry the same look of shock. We'll have a lot of explaining to do. Later.

Lucky turns to me and Thorne. "Shall we begin your first order of family business?"

Thorne looks to me. Mostly because his family business is completed. After all, Janais and Cole are now trapped together on a prison planet. *Cozy.* That leaves only one family business left undone.

Mine.

"I'm ready," I state.

The room falls silent as Luci and Conway step into the main chamber. They pause in the center of the room.

Luci lifts her shin. "You're going to kill us."

"No," I correct. "We're giving you a chance to aid the omniverse. You both have great skills. We'd like to put them to work."

Conway frowns. "What would we do?"

"Lucky showed me some visions," I state. "There are worlds in flux. These are not pleasant places, but you could do great good there."

Luci groans. "That sounds awful."

"We refuse," says Conway.

"So be it," states Thorne.

"Agreed." I focus on Luci and Conway. "Since you refuse to aid the emperor and empress, then your punishment shall be determined by another."

Lucky twiddles his fingers at Luci and Conway. "Hi, there."

Conway pales. "You can't punish us. You're the Sentient King."

"And you're an informed fellow," says Lucky.

"We change our minds," call Luci. "We'll serve the emperor and empress. Whatever."

"Too late," says Lucky. "Welcome to my world." The king snaps his fingers. Both Conway and Luci burst into a whirl of particles that move, pinwheel style, into ever smaller rounds. Within seconds, they disappear completely.

Ah, well. I gave them a chance.

"I guess that's all," I state. My gaze locks with Slate and Justice, who both look like the definitions of *miserable*. I shoot Thorne the side eye. "Or is there one last thing to do?"

"There is," replies Thorne.

At this moment, Chloe and Zoe step into the reception chamber. Upon spying Justice and Slate, they cheer. Within seconds, Justice has his arms around Zoe's waist and is swinging her about in big circles. Chloe and Slate stand face to face, their fingers entwined and foreheads touching.

Lucky then turns to address the entire court. "All hail, the sixth age of Umbra!"

Everyone bows.

And a new age does indeed begin.

"If one is lucky, visiting a parallel world ends in creating a new one." - Beauregard the Great, author of *Instructions for Visiting Parallel Worlds*

MEIMI and I ride hoverbikes through the red desert of Umbra. This is becoming a weekly ritual for us. It's a good way to break past the formalities of court. Not to mention the hard work of repairing space and time in the viz dome.

To honor our one month anniversary as emperor and empress, I have a special surprise set up for us both.

Juicing my speed, I take the lead on our journey. Our first stop? Tooling past the very place in the red desert where I saw the vision of me and Meimi riding by.

Long story short, I'm not sure which moment was the one where I detected Meimi and I riding by, one month and a million years ago. So we hit the spot on a regular basis.

Afterwards, I make sure Meimi rides along by my side as we speed toward my surprise—a hidden drift void.

We race through. The second we hit the hidden void, a flash of silver light surrounds us. One moment, we're in the red desert. The next, we're riding over the Pacific Ocean on Earth.

Meimi beams. "What was that?"

"A new invention of mine." I wink. "Hidden drift void. You can set them up and leave them for later use."

"Cool tech! Where's the next one?"

"Who says there's another?"

"I do."

I laugh. "And you're right."

Leaning to one side, I head off into a new direction. We flash through a quick succession of hidden drift voids, each one with a different destination.

There's Umbran's purple trenches.

Earth's Amazon jungle.

And finally, the blue beaches of Komandir.

Here, I force my hoverbike to stop. Meimi halts her vehicle beside mine.

"This place is gorgeous!" Slipping off the bike, she steps to my side. Linking her fingers with mine, Meimi guides me to the ground. "Get over here, emperor."

A fresh emotion pours through our transcendent bond—a flare of passion.

"As my empress commands."

And so, I step off onto the warm beach.

THORNE PRESSES his lips to mine. His mouth is all things warm, firm and perfect. Shocks of pleasure move though me.

Ah, my emperor.

A month ago, that title would have seemed impossible. Now I can't imagine Thorne as anything else.

Our kiss turns fierce. Thorne guides me down onto the smooth sands of this alien beach. The firm planes of his body press against my own.

"You know what to do," I whisper.

"That I do."

Thorne commands his sentient clothing to vanish. I do the same. Every inch of me lights up with desire, knowing we have no official duties today, other than enjoying time with each other.

It's true that Thorne and I may never have expected to become emperor and empress. Still—in this moment—it's the best outcome in the omniverse.

—

—The End—

ALSO BY CHRISTINA BAUER

Try ANGELBOUND, the kick-ass paranormal romance with more than
1 million copies sold!

FAIRY TALES OF THE MAGICORUM

A modern fairy tale that *USA Today* calls a 'must-read!' Check out WOLVES AND ROSES!

Medieval mages ... Slow-burn love ... And heart-pounding action! Check out the BEHOLDER series!

PIXIELAND DIARIES

PIXIELAND DIARIES tells the story of sassy pixie Calla and 'her' elf prince, Dare.

NEW APPENDIX OF TOTALLY AWESOME GOODIES

Welcome to this new appendix!

I've added lots of extra stuff here in order to celebrate the release of new covers for my Dimension Drift series! Check them out below:

Say it with me: *ooooh, aaaaaah!*

Now, you may wonder: *what's behind the new covers?*
Good question, you.
There are my five reasons why I did this.

One. The 'I Gotta Be Me' Cover

With the original covers, the first three had a theme of characters running through walls. Then the fourth book, ECHO ACADEMY, did it own thing. It was walls, walls, walls and... WTF? That bugged me.

Two. I Like Visuals

Reviewers often say that reading my books is like watching a movie in their heads. And hey, that's what it's like when I write them, too! Even after the books are launched, I'm still picturing the story and how to enhance it. All of which leads to item number three...

Three. More Books A-Coming

Great news! I plan on adding two more books to the series, namely JUSTICE and SLATE. As it was before, the cover design template wasn't really expandable to those guys. After all, you can only run through so many walls before things starts to get repetitive. This new format will fit in the two new titles perfectly. Yay!

Four. Getting Less Literal

The first covers represented actual scenes from the books. It was fun at the time, but I think it's a little limiting in the long run. Plus, this series is science fiction which I think lends itself to more *suggestive versus literal* design. The new look should give you an idea of the book's themes without getting too specific.

Four. Reader Goodies

Recently, I added an extra appendix to SLIPPERS AND THIEVES, a title from my Fairy Tales of the Magicorum series. Readers really liked it—and I love making you all happy—so the new covers were a good excuse to add in more content here as well.

All in all, I truly hope you enjoy these extra goodies... and please keep an eye out for a release date on JUSTICE and SLATE!

Best,
Christina Bauer, Author

CHECK out the top five things to know about the main character, Meimi Archer.

Fact Five.
Meimi lives in a dystopian version of Boston.

In this future, Boston is a domed city, meaning that it's safe and non-toxic and all that good stuff. outside of a dome, most of the continent is a shit show. Ruins. Toxic sludge. You get the idea.

Fact Four.
The Authority runs the show.

About twenty years ago, the Authority ousted the government of the United Americas. They're obsessed with purity in citizens and they purge anyone who doesn't meet their standards. And yes, purging means what you think it does. Murder.

Fact Three.
Meimi's Mother is slated for cleansing.

Rose Archer used to be a top researcher in drift science, but she's been slowly turning catatonic over the years. To protect her mom, Meimi moves out to Western Massachusetts and lives off grid in an abandoned factory. Which leads to..

Fact Two.
Meimi is a science genius.

Meimi's mother taught our heroine tons about drift science, and Meimi uses those skills to do build science gizmos for the local crime lord.

Fact one.
Meimi is also a geek.

Meimi is a wizard when it comes to drift science, but she's super awkward around guys her age. In fact, she's not comfortable around anyone but her best friends, Chloe and Zoe. That is, until a hottie extraterrestrial enters Meimi's life. And so the story goes!

HERE ARE profiles on five ECHO ACADEMY characters , as well as links to their inspiration boards on Pinterest!

Number Five.
Meimi Archer

If you've been following the series, you know what Meimi Archer was the main character in SCTHE, which was the prequel novella to UMBRA. Meimi is a science geek for hire in a dystopian version of Boston, MA. Our heroine builds gadgets for an underworld mob boss in order to keep herself (and her mother) safely hidden from the government.

Number Four.
The Authority

I build out character sheets and inspiration boards for key people in my worlds, but it rarely ends there. Key institutions also need to be fleshed out as well. This is true for the Authority, which is the new government that just took over in the United Americas. The Authority places all worthy citizens into domed cities, while undesirables are locked out and 'euthanized' in 'purges.'

Number Three.
Sentient

Sentient are also key characters in the book. They are minute cybernetic creatures that live inside people from the planet UMBRA. Sentient partially exist on the quantum level, so they have a unique view into time and space. They empower Umbran royals like Thorne with the ability to guard and garden the omniverse, the universe of universes.

Number Two.
Umbra, Thorne's home planet

The Planet Umbra is home to the royal family that guards the omniverse, so at first I wanted it to be super high-tech. But then I thought that, if you're REALLY high tech, you'd long for the days when the world looked organic. So I decided to make Umbra appear like an Old West planet, but actually everything there is made from high-tech filaments when you look closely enough.

Number One.
Prince Thorne

There are three royal brothers on Umbra, and Thorne's the middle child. Our hero is supposed to have tons of power over sentient, but he doesn't. Instead, Thorne tends to take great risks in guarding the omniverse—to the point where Thorne's older brother Justice thinks he has a death wish.

So there you have it—profiles of my top five characters for ECHO ACADEMY!

UNLESS YOU'RE a Tolkien freak like me, you may not be aware that there are actually three different versions of LOTR out there (2 film and 1 radio). As a public service, I have forthwith ranked them Bronze, Silver and Gold as follows:

The Bronze goes to...
The Cartoon LOTR

This animated version was released in 1978 complete with big-eyed Frodo, a badass Aragorn, and quite a few musical numbers, some of which are pretty catchy. It's worth a watch if you're an LOTR aficionado, or if you want to see how differently two film directors can reinterpret the same source material (or in some cases, how they can somehow choose the exact same shots!)

For me, the best part of this movie was Aragorn, pure and simple. No offense to Viggo, but in the books Aragon was no hottie, yet he was still super-attractive. The animated LOTR captures this concept handily. And why is that so important to me? Well, the cartoon below says it all:

And the Silver goes to...
The PJ LOTR

Now, we come to what many consider to be THE non-print version of LOTR.

Don't get me wrong, Peter Jackson and his interpretations of Tolkien will continue to separate me from my money for many years to come.

And *Fellowship of the Ring* was freaking phenomenal. I saw it in the theaters 13 times, and caught something new each visit. Look at the little flowers in the Shire gardens! Oooooh, there's the party tree! And WOW, the orcs look so cool! SQUEEEE!

If the next two movies had kept up that mind-blowing level of awesomeness, I would have been hard pressed not to give this one the Gold. But my favorite parts of the story were missing, and arguably there wasn't much Peter Jackson could do about it (more on that below.)

Which means the Gold goes to…
The BBC LOTR

In 1981, the BBC did a 13-part interpretation of LOTR as a radio play and MAN, does it ever KICK ASS.

IMHO, the reason's because LOTR was partially inspired by epic poems of the Beowulf ilk, so they're meant to be performed by a professional storyteller who sits before a roaring fire, weaving spine-tingling tales to an audience filled with mead, ill-gotten treasure, and huzzahs. There's nothing like having LOTR spoken aloud to bring out those primal, epic roots.

And that, my friends, means a radio play. Listen to this one; it's gorgeous!

WHAT ARE the top 10 items on my bucket list? Read on the find out.

Number 10.
See the Pyramids of Egypt. Since pyramids are cool.

Number 9.
Write 100 books. Just because I can. *Maybe*.

Number 8.
Eat my weight in pizza.
(I may have already reached this one)

Number 7.
Have a sandwich named after me.
(more food stuff, yeah!)

Number 6.
Never watch the movie *Bucket List*.

Number 5.
Bring *Huzzah* back as a catch phrase.

Number 4.
Get free spa treatments for life.

Number 3.

Never go on a cruise.
(I watched too much *Love Boat* as a kid, which ruined this for me.
Remember the episode with Ernest Borgnine? Yeah, that sucked.)

Number 2.

Tell those meddling kids to get off my lawn.

Number 1.

Grow gray hair down to my waist, wear long white dresses, and have
children call me Mrs B.
(That's really three things but I got inspired!)

STANDARD APPENDIX OF STUFF THAT'S STILL PRETTY COOL

IF YOU ENJOYED THIS BOOK...

...Please consider leaving a review, even if it's just a line or two. Every bit truly helps.

Plus I have it on good authority that every time you review an indie author, somewhere an angel gets a mocha latte.

For reals.

And angels need their caffeine, too.

ACKNOWLEDGMENTS

If you're reading my freaking acknowledgements, chances are, I should thank you for something. So, for the record: you are awesome, dear reader.

That said, huge and heartfelt thanks must go out to my husband and son for their rock-solid support. Being an author means a lot of early mornings, late nights, long weekends, and never-ending patience. You two are the best guys in the universe, period.

After that, I must thank the extensive network of reviewers, friends and colleagues who helped me build my writing chops in general. Gracias.

Finally, deep affection goes out to my late, much loved, and dearly missed Aunt Sandy and Uncle Henry. You saw the writer in me, always. Thank you, first and last.

ABOUT CHRISTINA BAUER

Christina Bauer thinks that fantasy books are like bacon: they just make life better. All of which is why she writes romance novels that feature demons, dragons, wizards, witches, elves, elementals, and a bunch of random stuff that she brainstorms while riding the Boston T. Oh, and she includes lots of humor and kick-ass chicks, too. Christina lives in Newton, MA with her husband, son, and semi-insane golden retriever, Ruby.

Stalk Christina on Social Media

Blog:
http://monsterhousebooks.com/blog/category/christina

Facebook:
https://www.facebook.com/authorBauer/

Instagram:
https://www.instagram.com/christina_cb_bauer/

Twitter:
@CB_Bauer

VLOG:
https://tinyurl.com/Vlogbauer

Web site:
www.bauersbooks.com

COMPLIMENTARY BOOK

Get a FREE book when you sign up for Christina's newsletter: https://tinyurl.com/bauersbooks

BEVERLY HILLS VAMPIRE

**A NOVELLA BY
CHRISTINA BAUER**

www.ingramcontent.com/pod-product-compliance
Lightning Source LLC
Chambersburg PA
CBHW032006170626

46807CB00006B/2679

9 7 8 1 9 4 5 7 2 3 4 8 3